WYVILLE
GLENN V. WYVILLE, age 64, devoted husband of Marilyn E. (nee Miller); dear father of Cynthia (Jack) Hancharick, Dale and Darren (Lynn); brother of Ralph; loving grandfather of Matthew and Kyle. Former teacher for 34 years and basketball coach for 28 years with the Chagrin Falls Schools. Summer Recreation Director for 24 years; Chairman of the Recreation Council; member of the United Methodist Church and the Village Shade Tree Commission. Avid gardener and fisherman. Other interests included woodworking, stamp collecting and watching the "Tribe." Friends may call at the Fireside Book Shop, 29 N. Franklin St. from 10:00 am to 8:30 pm. Monday through Sunday.

Calling Hours

Written by
Glenn Wyville

Published in the United States of America by
Fireside Book Shop
29 Franklin Street
Chagrin Falls Ohio
440.247.4050

Cover design and book layout/design by
Tag Art Studio 440.247.6990

Cover watercolor by
Marilyn Evans

First Edition
ISBN   0-9700846-0-9

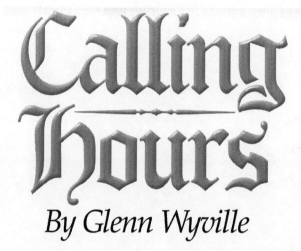

By Glenn Wyville

ACKNOWLEDGEMENTS

Since my retirement from Chagrin Falls Schools in 1991, I have been employed by Don Lawrence, owner of the Stroud-Lawrence Funeral Home. At the risk of sounding macabre, I must admit that this has been an enjoyable association. Those of you who are acquainted with Don know exactly what I mean. Our many discussions relating to various situations that have occurred over the years gave me the spark needed to attempt this endeavor. My thanks to Don for his technical advice and encouragement.

Several friends read the book in its various stages of development and seemed to like it. This response was appreciated, but I realized that I needed a more objective opinion. I approached Jim Lewis, owner of the Fireside Book Shop in Chagrin Falls, and asked him if he might have time to read it. Jim's years of experience would give me an indication as to whether I should pursue it to its conclusion since I had never done anything like this before. His opinion would be critical. He gladly agreed, and after reading what I had completed, gave me the encouragement to continue. He also gave me several key suggestions on how the book might be expanded through additional subplots.

It's sad that so many small community bookstores have been forced to close their doors due to competition from the large chains. I sincerely hope that day never comes to Chagrin Falls.

A special thanks to Scott Lax, a former student and author of "The Year that Trembled." He took time from his busy schedule to provide valuable advice.

Last, but by no means least, the final and most essential ingredient. Like most people who had never had a piece of work published, I had no clue as to the importance of an editor. I can now say that without the tireless efforts of Susi Tedrick, this book would not have become a reality. An author creates a story, but an editor creates the book.

To Marilyn

Not only my secretary, but my most severe critic, both of which were indispensable. My gratitude is only surpassed by my love.

Prologue

CLEVELAND CLINIC
SPRING, 1975

He lay back on the bed with his hands clasped behind his head. "What a sweetheart deal. They hide me in this hospital, feed and protect me, and then I drop the bomb on those bastards."

There was a faint trace of a smile across his face. "I'm going to be rich," he thought. He'd be somebody; he'd have the respect that they had never shown him. His features slowly turned into a sadistic sneer. "They'll be sorry," he hissed. "I'll bring them all down." He closed his eyes, daydreaming of sweet revenge.

In the basement cafeteria an orderly carefully loaded dinner trays on a tall serving cart. He finished and wheeled the cart toward the elevator. As the door opened he heaved a quick sigh of relief. So far so good - it was empty.

He pushed the button for the fifth floor and nervously waited for the doors to close. As he glanced up at the numbers above him, the second floor light came on. A confident grin appeared. "Everything is going according to plan," he said out loud to no one in particular.

The elevator stopped at two. A short, muscular man in an orderly's uniform stepped in. Their eyes met. The first man held out his hand, and a slip of paper was pressed into it as the second man stepped back into the hall. The numbers "505" were written on it. He crumpled it and put it in his pocket as the doors closed.

The elevator stopped as it reached the fifth floor. He pushed the cart out into the hall and nervously gazed down its length. Room 505 was easy to spot. A policeman sat with his chair tilting precariously against the wall. He was reading a magazine outside the door. It would be the orderly's third stop.

He approached Room 501, carefully removed a tray and entered the room. He placed the tray on the small table without saying a word to the patient. After giving a forced nod and a nervous smile, he was back out into the hall. His heart was beating rapidly, and he could feel his face beginning to flush. He repeated the same procedure in Room 503 and cautiously approached 505. The policeman raised his head slightly and gave him a brief disinterested look before returning to his magazine.

Just as the orderly was about to enter the room, the policeman spoke. "Wait a second," he called.

The orderly's hand instinctively moved toward the bulge under his belt in the middle of his back; then he forced himself to relax. His heart was beating so loudly he was afraid it could be heard at the other end of the hall.

"I almost forgot," the policeman continued. "I'm supposed to check everyone and everything entering this room." He glanced at the stocky man's ID tag and picture. "Oh, what the hell; you look harmless enough. Go on in. Hard to tell if hospital food's poisoned anyway." He laughed at his own lame attempt to be humorous.

The orderly's right hand returned to the cart as he gave a forced laugh. "It was almost over before it even started," he thought to himself. He quickly turned, fearing the perspiration he felt beading up on his forehead would become evident.

He removed the tray and slowly opened the door. His head was down as he quietly entered and closed the door behind him. The room was dark except for the pulsation of light coming from the television set facing the bed. The silent screen cast an eerie glow across the bed and its occupant. He had hoped for a little background noise, but this would have to do.

The man in the bed lay quietly, his hands clasped behind his head. His eyes were still closed. As the orderly placed the tray gently on the table, the patient opened his eyes. His face contorted in fear as he recognized his visitor. Before he could utter a sound, his assassin forced a pillow over his face and produced a gun with a silencer attached.

Two sharp reports into the pillow and the struggling ceased. Crimson circles appeared and began enlarging on the pillow's surface. He quickly felt for any sign of life in his victim. Finding none, he covered the lifeless form with the sheet and moved toward the door. He failed to notice that the dead man's finger was on the buzzer.

He left the room, drawing little more than an acknowledging nod from the policeman, and proceeded down the hall. Two more stops and he could slip through the exit door to safety.

As he was leaving the last room, he heard a loud scream coming from 505. The policeman jumped to his feet as a nurse ran into the hall screaming and waving her arms wildly. The policeman turned and rushed down the hall with his pistol drawn. He was yelling something, but the assassin could not hear.

Alerted by the screams and the onrushing policeman, he crashed against the exit door and began descending the stairs three and four at a time. His accomplice would be at the hospital's entrance in a car with the motor running. If he could just make it to the car, they had a good chance of escaping.

He hit the third floor landing with a violent crash as his left leg buckled. Pain shot up his leg as he felt himself beginning to black out. No matter how much it hurt, he could not allow himself to slow down. When he reached the second floor, the pain was almost more than he could bear. He stopped to listen. Other footsteps began echoing in the stairwell.

"Just one more floor and safety," he gasped in agony. Somehow he reached the first floor and headed for the exit, dragging his twisted leg. He crashed through the door and saw the car waiting. He pulled the door open and collapsed into the front seat. He was exhausted, and the searing pain in his leg left him immobile.

"Go!" he screamed as he twisted toward the driver. His labored breathing stopped when he saw the seat was unoccupied. And no key in the ignition.

He sat in silence and leaned his head against the dashboard, resigning himself to his fate. By this time, the car was being surrounded by cautiously approaching hospital security guards. As sirens moaned in the background, he was dimly aware of what was happening. His eyes rolled back as in a voice barely audible, he sobbed, "Goodbye my dearest Rosalie; goodbye my beautiful son. I love you."

1

CLEVELAND FBI HEADQUARTERS
OCTOBER, 1998

Tony sat there wondering how in the world he had ever allowed himself to end up in this situation. He wished the past months could be programmed right out of his life. It seemed like 100 years ago as his mind drifted back to that sunny June day just over four months ago.

"We will provide you with a new passport, driver's license, birth certificate and social security number. We'll be transporting you to your new location right after the trial." The voice of special agent Ben Griffin snapped Tony back to reality.

"How long do you think the trial will last?" Tony asked dejectedly.

"It's hard to tell," said Ben. "Sometimes they can drag on for months - depends on how skillful the defense is at stalling tactics and evading the issues. With you as our star witness, we should be able to tie this up a lot sooner. An eyewitness account can do more to convince a jury than anything their slick-talking consigliere can contrive. Of course, we can count on professional witnesses attempting to discredit your testimony."

"Great," said Tony, his voice oozing with sarcasm. "I can't wait to begin my new life. I'm really looking forward to moving somewhere I've never even heard of and never seeing my home and friends again. Isn't there any other way we can do this?" he pleaded. "The witness protection program seems so drastic."

"It's all been explained to you, Tony. We've gone over this time and time again. When you agreed to help us, you knew what the downside would be. Anyway, I'm afraid it's too late to change your mind now. At this point it wouldn't matter. If you were out on the street, you wouldn't live to see the next sunrise."

Tony knew he was right - there was no turning back now. The sooner he resigned himself to it the sooner he could get on with his new identity. Even though he'd be with his family, it was little consolation. He felt guilty at having to uproot them. He could cope with taking Mama away - she would be happy anywhere as long as it was with him. However, it was a different story for his uncle and cousins.

Uncle Gino was the only father he had ever known. Though he was a kind and thoughtful man, it was just not the same. It was always "Uncle Gino" and never "Dad".

Albert, Frankie and Tony were all within three years of one another and had lived under the same roof for most of their lives. That was where the similarities ended. It was not to say that they didn't get along. They remained close even now that their lives were so removed from his. Albert and Frankie had simply followed a different direction and were quite content. They had chosen not to attend college and joined the work force immediately after graduation from high school. Albert was the produce manager at Russo's Supermarket and Frankie had worked his way up to assistant chef at Gamekeeper's. They were an integral part of the community, firmly entrenched in the everyday life of the Village.

They were bound to resent being exiled, and he couldn't blame them one bit. Life had certainly become complicated, but at least he was still on the green side of the grass. There were several times during the past few months when his chances of survival had seemed slim at best. He rationalized that after what he'd been through, each new day was a gift for which he should be extremely grateful.

THE OHIO STATE UNIVERSITY
EARLY MAY, 1998

Tony sat in the long row. The spring sun beat down on his robe, creating a one-man sauna. As the speaker droned on, his mind began drifting back to earlier times and the people who had made it possible for him to be sitting here today.

He thought of Mama, whose main purpose in life had been to provide the stability of a loving home. She had willingly given up so much for him. He wondered what his life might have been like if his father had lived. Would he have wanted to become a mortician? Would he even have gone to college? Though he was very happy to be where he was today, he couldn't help but feel a tinge of regret for what might have been.

He thought how lucky he was to have had a substitute father like his uncle Gino. Uncle Gino had generously shared his time and energy between his own two sons and Tony. There were many occasions when questions were better answered by someone other than Mama, and Uncle Gino had always been there for him. How often had he benefited from the advice he provided? More than he could ever begin to count.

He recalled the day he had timidly approached Don Lawrence and asked if there were odd jobs he might do at the funeral home. Don had seen a shy, somewhat introverted boy and set out to provide him with an identity and a purpose. From that day on, Tony's life had changed.

As he glanced in the direction of his wonderful family, he couldn't help but notice a white-haired old man sitting a few rows behind Mama. He seemed to be staring right through her directly into Tony's eyes. Tony strained to recall the face that seemed distantly familiar. He felt he knew him, but when and from where?

Just as he was about to return his attention to the stage, the old man nodded his head and a trace of a smile creased his wrinkled features.

This brief encounter ended abruptly as his row stood and began proceeding toward the platform.

He reached the bottom of the steps. He heard his name announced: "Anthony Amico." As he approached the podium to receive his diploma, a loud cheer came from a small group seated in the front row. Tony's eyes darted toward the sound, and a wide grin split his face. The look of pride on their faces made the last six years worthwhile. There was Mama, standing, beaming and crying. Uncle Gino was jumping up and down, waving his arms frantically. The source of the noise came from his cousins, Albert and Frankie. Since they were twice the size of normal people, it only figured they would create considerable racket.

A little more subdued, but every bit as proud, sat Don and Judi Lawrence. They owned the Stroud-Lawrence Funeral Home in Tony's hometown of Chagrin Falls. Their encouragement and guidance were instrumental in directing him toward the achievement of his goal. Don displayed the thumbs-up sign as Judi blew him a kiss. Unfortunately, their busy schedule only allowed them time enough to attend the commencement ceremony. Tony realized this and looked directly at them. His lips parted as he smiled and mouthed, "Thank you for everything." Don brushed a tear from the corner of his eye.

"What an old softy. Your tear ducts must be attached directly to your bladder," Judi teased as she deftly applied a quick dab of Kleenex to her eyes before her mascara started running.

They were up and gone before the ceremony's conclusion. Don had to meet with a family at three-thirty back in Chagrin Falls. It would be close. This was typical of the plight of a funeral director, especially when operating with a small staff. Judi eagerly anticipated the time when Tony would be able to take some of the pressure off her beleaguered husband. Don always said jokingly, "If business is slow, all I have to do is plan a vacation. Then the phone will start ringing off the wall." Sad but true, it was more often the case than not.

———≫•◦•≪———

Tony Amico was twenty-four going on forty. His dark curly hair was cut very short, giving him a military look. At five feet ten inches, he supported that military look with a straight upright carriage. His stocky build enhanced the image. As a youngster he was described as pudgy. In high school his classmates jokingly called him "The Pillsbury Dough Boy." This label was misleading. He was anything but soft, physically or mentally.

The only child of a single parent, he had developed a positive work ethic at a young age. This quality had enabled him to hold a job and keep his grade point at 3.75. Though he was well liked, his no-nonsense attitude had made him somewhat of a loner. Friendly, but by no means outgoing, he had been more serious than most teenagers were. His refusal to do the crazy things typical of his peers had kept him from developing close friendships. Traditional activities such as the annual Pumpkin Roll, Senior Cut Day, and "cruising" had not been part of his agenda.

Sports were an essential part of school life at Chagrin Falls High. Being an athlete automatically insured one's popularity. Social life centered on "the games," its participants and the parties that followed.

There had been no doubt in anyone's mind that, had he chosen to do so, Tony could have been a fine athlete and an esteemed member of the "in crowd." Coaches and students had constantly exhorted him to go out for "the team." Their urgings had been met with a polite refusal.

After awhile only the most steadfast had continued the quest. Coaches, the most insightful, had also been the most persistent. They had seen qualities in Tony that they hoped for in all their athletes, but seldom were fortunate to realize. He had an aura about him - one of quiet dignity. Coaches had drooled when they thought of the leadership, if only by example, he could have brought to a team.

In the winter of his sophomore year, Coach Wem - who had also been his gym teacher - finally convinced him to go out for wrestling. Coach was a bear of a man - not someone anyone would ever wish to anger. But in truth, he was more like a big teddy bear. Tony had had great affection for this soft-spoken, easy-going giant. Everyone who had known Coach Wem also knew of his ability to exercise his vocal chords. Other coaches had shaken their heads and agreed that if anyone could wear Tony down, it had to be Coach Wem.

True to his nature, Tony had worked hard and never missed a practice. He had been serious about his commitment and improved steadily. Toward the end of the season he had even participated in two varsity contests. Through it all, Coach Wem had grudgingly sensed this would be Tony's first and only wrestling experience. Tony had said he would do it and was not about to quit, but it was obvious his heart was not in it. This didn't stop Coach Wem from unsuccessfully trying to persuade Tony to participate each year thereafter. He had lamented to anyone who would listen that Tony Amico was definitely State qualifying material.

Tony had dated in high school, but he had never had time to allow a serious relationship to develop. He had attended the essential things like proms and formals, but it seemed more of an obligation than going for the sheer fun of it. He hadn't been anti-social, but one had always sensed there was a line he would not cross. As a result, Tony had missed out on many things that others might consider frivolous simply because asking him had always resulted in a polite refusal. Yes, Tony had had his priorities, but sadly he had missed the opportunity to just be a typical kid. If this fact bothered him, it was not evident to anyone.

Through it all, Tony had had one driving ambition - to provide financial security for Mama. Though in her late forties, the years of sacrifice had not destroyed her natural beauty. Uncle Gino had often said, "Your mama was the prettiest girl in all of Little Italy. Bella donna," he called her.

Tony remembered asking her why she had never remarried. "Mama, I think you should find a good man and get married again," he once told her. "I really wouldn't mind; you deserve some happiness. You've given so much to all of us."

"Why do I need another man when I have a beautiful son like you?" was her reply. "No one could make me any happier." She seemed perfectly satisfied with her role. Mama had doted on everyone in the family, but he was special, and Tony vowed to make it up to her one day.

He had worked for Stroud-Lawrence Funeral Home in some capacity since he was ten years old. Beginning with yard work, washing vehicles and a variety of odd jobs, more and more responsibility was thrust upon him. He had efficiently handled each new task and became their most reliable part-time employee. It had been obvious Tony enjoyed the type of work that most teenagers avoided like the plague. Don Lawrence had constantly encouraged Tony to give a career in the mortuary business serious consideration. He had never met someone as mature and dependable at such a young age.

Tony felt great admiration for Don. Besides being his mentor, he considered Don a loyal friend. Tony had carefully watched this man's skill at readily sharing a warm laugh or a heartfelt tear. Don had an uncanny sense of timing, allowing him to say just the right thing at the appropriate time. Watching Don bring a smile or even a laugh through a flood of tears from a mourner never ceased to amaze Tony. Don made people feel comfortable by sharing their grief with a sincere compassion. Naturally, those people skills didn't just develop overnight, and Tony fervently hoped someday to be just like Don.

The Lawrences had often included Tony in functions outside the funeral home business. Don would continually implore him to "get that sheepskin."

"I need a good Italian stallion to draw some business away from my competition. But if I ever hear that you're even thinking of going to another 'home', I'll place a call to some friends of mine. They'll bring me your genitals in a jar. I'll embalm them and keep them on my desk. Then instead of the 'Italian Stallion' they can call you the 'Neutered Neapolitan'."

Sometime during his junior year of high school, Tony had told Mama that he wanted to attend college and pursue a career as a mortician. She hadn't been surprised by his announcement. She had told him that money was available should he decide to further his education. She had explained she had been putting small amounts away ever since he was a child.

Upon entering The Ohio State University, he had never wavered from his goal. After six years of hard work, he was now proudly receiving his degree in mortuary science with a minor in criminology. His second career choice, that of a law enforcement officer, was his backup just in case he didn't like the life of a mortician.

At the conclusion of the ceremony, Tony rushed to his family and hugged Mama. The others pounded his back, pumped his hand and waited for their chance to kiss both his cheeks in the traditional manner.

Tony scanned the crowd for a closer look at the old man, but he was gone so Tony turned his full attention to the excitement of the moment.

———⊱•◦•⊰———

Standing an appropriate distance away, observing the festivities, was an interested stranger. After giving the group a chance to allow their exuberance to subside, the stranger approached Tony. He was a tall, distinguished-looking man of about fifty. Cleanly shaven, with black hair combed straight back that showed no sign of graying, he had a presence that demanded one's full attention. His heavy dark eyebrows were arched, giving him a demonic appearance. His dark suit was obviously expensive and well tailored. He wore gold on both hands, but it was not gaudy. As he extended a well-manicured hand, he introduced himself, speaking with a slight accent.

"Hello, Tony. My name is Carlo Bonitto. I represent Good Shepherd Funeral Home in Cleveland, Ohio. Let me congratulate you on your graduation."

"Mr. Bonitto, I am really honored that a prestigious establishment like Good Shepherd would send you to see me," Tony responded.

Good Shepherd was arguably the finest funeral home in the Midwest. Its former employees could form a "Who's Who" of successful morticians. Each year only one or two graduates were chosen for the necessary two-year apprenticeship. Two years at Good Shepherd carried an automatic invitation to join practically any funeral home in the country.

Don had encouraged him to do his apprenticeship somewhere other than Stroud-Lawrence. He and Judy eagerly anticipated the day Tony could take some of the pressure off the one-man operation. But from a business standpoint, Don felt Tony would benefit from experiences gained at another establishment. "What a stroke of luck," thought Tony. "Good Shepherd." He could not suppress his grin, and he didn't even care to try.

"May I call you 'Tony'?" Bonitto asked. Smiling ever so slightly but not waiting for an answer, he continued. "Tony, we would like to fly you to Cleveland for an interview. As you know, an apprenticeship is normally not a high paying job. However, I think you'll find our offer quite generous. We have a private jet scheduled to depart at eight o'clock tomorrow morning. I hope this isn't rushing you too much," Bonitto said almost apologetically.

"I've worked practically all my life for this opportunity. Believe me, you are not rushing me at all," beamed Tony, still pumping his hand vigorously.

"Good," said Bonitto, finally withdrawing his hand from Tony's enthusiastic grasp. "If you will give me your address, our limousine will pick you up at seven tomorrow morning. Once again, please accept our congratulations on what you have accomplished." He handed Tony his card and quickly parted with, "This is only the beginning, my young friend."

When Tony told Mama about his conversation with Bonitto, she wasn't as happy as he had expected. Instead, she cast a worried glance toward Uncle Gino. Uncle Gino slapped Tony on the back and hugged him again, drawing Tony's attention away from his mother's concerned gaze. Mama quickly regained her composure.

<hr />

Tony's mother had refused to talk about the father he'd never known. Through the years when he had questioned her, she would always change the subject. On those rare occasions, she had abruptly dismissed his query with, "He died in an accident when you were very young. That's all you need to know." He had realized it was hopeless to pursue, and for the most part, the subject seldom came up. However, the question had nagged him through the years. He had never understood her refusal to talk about his father. What deep, dark secrets had caused her to stubbornly insulate him from his past?

To his knowledge there were no aunts, uncles or cousins on his father's side in this country. It was as if his father had not existed, and Tony was the only evidence that he actually had. Uncle Gino, his mother's only brother, was even less help. He would get very defensive when Tony asked him about his brother-in-law and seemed almost afraid to talk about him. It had been evident there was something in the past that no one wished to discuss.

Tony's frustration had pushed for answers, but none had been forthcoming.

The only other bit of information he had grudgingly obtained was that they had once lived in the part of Cleveland known as Little Italy and had moved from there when he was very young. Tony had grown up in Chagrin Falls and had no recollection of anything before that. Someday, he vowed, he would have the answers he wanted.

After a royal feast at Vito Gallo's Italian Gardens, the Amico family continued their celebration over wine and cappuccino. There was much laughter and singing. Some college friends joined the small group to offer congratulations. Mama seemed a little subdued through it all, but Tony attributed it to the strain of the long day's activities. Finally he reluctantly excused himself, stressing his early departure for Cleveland, kissed Mama, hugged Uncle Gino and his cousins, and was out the door. He felt like this had been the happiest day of his life.

Later, back at his apartment, Tony packed. Uncle Gino would be there later the next day to pick up everything Tony had accumulated over the past six years.

When his belongings were either in boxes or his suitcase, Tony tried unsuccessfully to sleep. It was impossible. The day's events and especially the unexpected visitor kept flooding his mind. The same questions kept coming back to him - Why me? Tony was a good student, but not exceptional. There were many with better qualifications. Were others contacted first and, for some reason, refused? Was there something about Good Shepherd he didn't know? Too late now, he'd have to go and listen to their offer. "Who knows - maybe they won't like me anyway," he rationalized.

He glanced at the clock - four a.m. "Great," he thought. "I won't have to worry about impressions - I'll be too tired to make one." As he finally drifted off to sleep, his last thought was "Why me"?

⋙•◦•⋘

The alarm painfully informed Tony that he had actually been sleeping. He doubted it could have been more than a few minutes. Maybe a shower would have the same therapeutic effect that it had while cramming for exams.

There is something to be said for being twenty-four years old, or maybe it was just nervous energy. For whatever reason, he felt surprisingly good. By the time the limo arrived, he was packed and ready to go.

The driver took the suitcase and opened the door to an empty car. "Where's Bonitto?" he wondered. "Probably he'll meet me at the plane."

The driver did not speak during the entire trip to Port Columbus, and Tony was too intimidated to speak first. When they arrived at the airport, the driver took his bags from the trunk and led him to the gate where the private plane waited.

He boarded the plane, and to his astonishment, he was the only passenger. No one greeted him nor spoke to him. It was like a ghost ship. He visualized going to the pilot's cabin and seeing no one at the controls.

The flight took only forty minutes. When the plane arrived at Cuyahoga County Airport, another empty limo with a non-verbal driver was waiting for him. He wanted so much to talk to somebody, but the driver gave him no encouragement.

"This day is sure not starting out the way I thought it would," he said to himself. "I hope this is not an omen."

Good Shepherd Funeral Home had been established in the early 1920's in a well-to-do area on the East Side of Cleveland. The name "Good Shepherd" was a deviation from the more common practice of naming an establishment after a family or families' surname (like Stroud-Lawrence).

Founded by three brothers who emigrated from Sicily in 1917 - Caesare, Anthony and Cosmo Scarletto - it was the largest funeral home serving the East Side. The building was magnificent, and the staff was excellent. Money, which was scarce in those days, did not seem to be a problem in developing the business.

The Scarletto brothers were not involved in the day-to-day operations, and in fact, were seldom seen. They employed professionals who gave no hint of any ethnic preference. For this reason, people of all nationalities felt comfortable using their services, and business flourished. Four funerals could be held simultaneously with no contact between the different mourning groups. The very wealthy to the poorest immigrant availed themselves of Good Shepherd's services with equal satisfaction.

The Scarlettos were phantoms who ran the business from an enigmatic, secluded world. Their walled estate on Murray Hill functioned like a fortress. Their children, and later grandchildren, were strangers to the staff of Good Shepherd. In fact, the only contact between the staff and the Scarletto Family was through Carlo Bonitto.

As the limo came over a small hill, the grounds of Good Shepherd came into full view. Tony gasped. He'd never seen a more impressive funeral home in his life.

The driver pulled under the portico as a great door swung open. A tall smiling man, probably in his late thirties, appeared. He remained on the porch gazing down at Tony with his arms folded. He was very impressive and dressed in the same elegant fashion as Carlo Bonitto. "In fact," thought Tony, "he looks a lot like Bonitto - enough to be a younger brother." The most striking feature was his hair - the color and sheen of motor oil and not one strand out of place. "I'll bet he could stand in the teeth of a hurricane and never have a single hair out of place. I'd love to see what it looks like in the morning. Probably just like it does now."

Tony, who had a tendency to look somewhat disheveled at times, could not help but be impressed with this man. Like Bonitto, he was impeccably dressed. His suit looked as though every square inch had been tailored to perfection. "If they can't teach me to be an undertaker, maybe they can at least teach me how to dress," he thought.

"Welcome to Good Shepherd," he said cheerily. "I'm Joshua Benitt, the general manager." He thrust out his hand and grasped Tony's with a strong handshake. "I trust you had a good trip. Congratulations on your graduation yesterday."

"Glad to meet you, Mr. Benitt," said Tony. "The trip went well and thanks, it's great to be finally emancipated."

"Please," said Benitt, "call me Josh. We're all one big family here. We hope to convince you to become a part of it. If you don't mind, I'd like to take you on a quick tour of the facility. Then we can sit down, relax over lunch and get down to specifics."

"That sounds great," agreed Tony. "How can you possibly take a 'quick' tour of this place," he thought to himself.

The building was unusual. However, it was perfectly suited for its purpose. From the air it probably looked like a miniature Pentagon. Four of the wings had a semi-circular drive coming off a larger drive that completely encircled the huge building. Within each semi-circular drive was a fountain with benches and beautiful landscaping. Expensive statuary was strategically located which gave the setting a feeling of tranquillity.

Four wings were almost identical, at least outwardly. The fifth one at the rear of the complex had an immense parking lot bounded by identical two-story buildings directly across the lot from one another. The lower level stabled the various vehicles. The second story housed apartments, two to each building.

At the rear of the lot stood a low brick structure, almost completely concealed by tall evergreen hedges. If one did not pay special attention, it could easily be overlooked. Three smokestacks at the rear identified its purpose - Good Shepherd's crematorium.

As impressive as the outside may have been, the inside was even more so. The wings were tastefully decorated, each in a different period. From this scheme, each section derived its means of identification. The Colonial wing was outfitted in Early American. Remaining were the French, English, and Modern wings. The rear annex contained the offices, a small cafeteria, meeting rooms, a large casket room and a spacious room where the deceased were skillfully prepared for viewing. This was referred to as the "prep" room.

Having the parking lot in the rear presented no problem logistically. Every driver entering the main gate was directed to the appropriate wing. As he or she pulled up to the portico, a valet assisted them from their car and parked the vehicle in the rear lot. Adequate drivers for the valet service were always available to accommodate the crowds.

The older men doubled as limo, hearse and escort drivers during funerals. Funerals in the various wings were staggered at half-hour intervals. No matter how well attended, calling hours were handled with the same competent efficiency. Their unusual system of valet parking was flawless.

"Well, what do you think of our 'little' neighborhood funeral home?" asked Josh with a slight touch of humor in his tone.

"Like the Grand Canyon, you have to see it in person to really appreciate its splendor," retorted Tony. "It must have cost a small fortune when it was built, another fortune to maintain and yet another to employ a staff. You must have a lot of funerals or a rich uncle."

Josh quickly dismissed his appraisal.

"We're quite busy as you might expect," responded Josh with no further explanation. "Now let's get some lunch and talk business."

Instead of going to the cafeteria, they entered one of the small conference rooms. A lunch was brought in by a member of the kitchen staff and placed on the table.

Josh began. "The success of any business depends on hiring good people. We do extensive research on all prospective employees. It might surprise you to know that we've been following your progress for quite some time."

"That's very flattering," said an amazed Tony. "But what's so special about me?"

"We don't just look into one's academic record," continued Josh. "We want individuals who have other qualities like loyalty and a good attitude. We want people who don't look at this as just a job but rather as a great opportunity. We want people with ambition who are willing to be good soldiers. We feel we know you well enough to know that you will not disappoint us. We are a bit unusual in that we don't require references. We feel more confidence in our own people's ability to make decisions."

"Boy, they must know things about me that I don't even know," thought Tony as he waited for Josh to continue.

"We like to have our apprentices living on the

grounds," said Josh. "You could be called upon to perform duties at any time of the day or night. Of course, this means that room and board are included in the financial package. You would not receive an hourly wage, but instead a salary that would net $3,000 a month."

"That's a very generous offer considering I'd have no out-of-pocket expenses," said Tony, trying not to appear overeager.

"We feel you are just the type of man we look for, and we hope that you give our offer strong consideration," said Josh.

"Where do I sign and when do I start?" asked Tony, no longer able to contain his enthusiasm.

Josh produced a legal-looking document and said, "We're pleased that you want to become a part of our Good Shepherd family. I've taken the liberty of having a contract drawn up, but I'd like you to take some time and read it over carefully. There are some stipulations that you should be aware of before signing. Please plan on staying the night. Then you can go over the contract carefully at your leisure."

Dinner would be at six so Tony had enough time to go over the contract in the privacy of his room. Like the rest of what he had previously seen, the quarters were equally well appointed. Tony assumed this was where he would live should he decide to stay.

The suite was completely furnished. It included a small but efficient kitchen, a combination living/dining room, a door that opened into a small bedroom and an adjacent bathroom. Tony had never been in an apartment more complete and elegantly furnished.

He sat at the dining room table and began studying the contract. The first portion contained what Josh had already discussed with him. The second portion grabbed his attention. The more he read, the more he felt like he would be signing away any vestige of a private life. For example, if he left the grounds for personal reasons, he was to sign out at the gate. Not only did he have to sign out, but he was required to stipulate destinations, estimated return time and phone numbers. No one was to be brought to his room unless Josh or his assistant were previously informed and had given their O.K.

"Why the secrecy?" he thought. As much as he wanted to start his career here, he would need some answers before signing the contract.

Tony did not see Josh at supper so he would have to wait until morning to get his answers. There were six others in the cafeteria by the time Tony arrived. Each person introduced himself and then returned to his table. Everyone seemed quite pleasant, but they gave the impression that they would not welcome additional conversation. There was little conversation even among them. "Bizarre," thought Tony, "they act like strangers."

After dinner he returned to his room. It had been a long day so he showered and decided to turn in early. He didn't anticipate staying awake long enough to get too involved in a program so he began "surfing" the channels with the remote. He stopped abruptly as an item on a local news channel caught his attention.

The report concerned a witness who was scheduled to testify before the grand jury but had mysteriously disappeared two days earlier. There had not been any clues, and as a result, the trial of a high-profile mobster had been put in jeopardy. The racketeer's name was Arnold Scarletto. The report went on to say that Scarletto was a nephew of the Scarletto Family, prominent businessmen on Cleveland's East Side. Without this witness the state had no case and would be forced to release Mr. Scarletto.

A slight breeze drifted through the open window causing an almost imperceptible shiver to course through his body. In the next instant he dropped the remote and fell asleep in the chair.

———⇒≫•◦•≪⇐———

Sleep would have been less peaceful had the news item probed more deeply into the history of the family who had just hired him. The Scarlettos were rumored to have strong underworld ties going all the way back to the days in Sicily. Several times in the last thirty years law enforcement officials had felt there was sufficient evidence for an indictment. Each time that "evidence" failed to materialize. As a result, there had never been a trial directly involving the Family.

Over the years several individuals who might have supplied evidence had disappeared without a trace. Although rumors persisted, the Family was relatively untouched by scandal, and apparently business did not suffer. The Scarlettos remained "prominent businessmen." There was little written or spoken that tied the Scarletto Family to Good Shepherd Funeral Home.

Tony went to breakfast refreshed and eager to meet with Josh. That is, if a few questions could be answered to his satisfaction. He had fallen asleep the previous night without calling Don Lawrence for his spin on Good Shepherd.

Josh appeared at his table and asked him to come to the conference room as soon as he had finished. He left the cafeteria. A few minutes later Tony followed and was knocking at the door.

"Come in, Tony," said a familiar voice.

He entered. Standing at the table was Carlo Bonitto. "Tony," he began, "we meet again. I'm sorry I couldn't accompany you here, but a pressing business matter forced me to leave prematurely. I trust Joshua has provided you with all the necessary information for you to make a decision." Bonitto was as imposing as he had been when they had met previously. Tony had to admit to being more than just a bit intimidated. Bonitto's demeanor left no doubt that he was in control. There was something about him that bordered on sinister. At best he could be characterized as dark and distant. There was little warmth in his voice even when he was trying to be cordial.

"Yes," answered Tony haltingly, "but I was wondering about the stipulations in the second part of the contract. Otherwise your offer is more than generous."

"Your concerns are valid and can easily be answered. Hopefully, they can be explained to your satisfaction," said Bonitto. "As it was stated in the contract, you may be called upon day or night if necessary. For this reason, should an emergency arise, we have to know how to get in touch with you quickly. You should know by now that our business demands immediate response to the needs of our customers."

"Of course," said Tony apologetically. "I should have realized that."

"As for the second matter," continued Bonitto, "it's not so easily explained. I guess you might say it's important for us to be aware of anyone coming here who would be close to the inner workings of our business. When one is successful, there are those for whom jealousy knows no bounds. We have no real secrets, but we like to defend our uniqueness."

Tony looked a bit puzzled at this vague explanation.

"I realize this may seem paranoid to you," said Bonitto, "but as time goes on, you will come to realize we have just cause asking this of our staff."

Tony did not feel his question had been sufficiently answered, but he was not about to question someone so imposing at the risk of being labeled a troublemaker before he'd even started.

"Mr. Bonitto, I would be pleased to become an employee of Good Shepherd," said Tony. He put out his hand and gave Bonitto's a firm shake. He then proceeded to sign the contract.

"Good," said Bonitto. "Take one of our vans back home to load your personal belongings. Be prepared to begin first thing Monday morning. I must warn you that you will be kept extremely busy. There will be little opportunity for socializing and even less time for trips home. You are here to help us, and we are here to help you. When your tenure is completed, we will both have benefited. With that in mind, let me be the first to officially welcome you to Good Shepherd family." Before Tony could respond, Bonitto turned and left the room.

Though somewhat bewildered, Tony was a happy man. He was anxious to get home and tell everyone the good news. Sure, he was going to miss his family, but it wasn't that far from home. Surely he'd have time off to visit them sometime. And this was exactly what he needed to fulfill his career goals. Who knew, someday it might be the Stroud-Lawrence-Amico Funeral Home - the best Chagrin Falls could offer.

The closer he got to Chagrin the more he began wondering how Mama would take the news. He clearly recalled her less than enthusiastic reaction. It was obvious if she had these reservations there must be a connection with the past. Once she was resigned to the fact that he was working for Good Shepherd, there was a chance she just might open up. He might finally get some answers to his questions. Could Good Shepherd be the key that would give him the peace of mind he so eagerly sought, or were the answers better left unknown?

"It's a beautiful day; enjoy the moment. This isn't a time to be thinking negative thoughts. Sit back and relax, you jerk."

As he pulled into the drive of their modest South Street home, everyone rushed out to greet him - except one.

"Where's Mama? In the kitchen?" asked Tony. He answered his own question. "Naturally. You cousins wouldn't look this way if she didn't spend so much time in there." Everyone laughed as they entered the house. Still, Tony thought it strange that she couldn't tear herself away long enough to join the others. But there she was - in her usual spot, cooking spaghetti sauce and who knows what other treats. The aromas of delicious concoctions filled the small kitchen.

"It's a wonder the linoleum isn't worn out in front of that stove," thought Tony as he rushed up, hugged her and smothered her with kisses. Mama eagerly returned his affectionate greeting, and Tony felt relieved.

"I miss you already," she said, wiping the tears from her eyes. "Now sit down and tell me all about it. Here's some kuchen, baked fresh this morning, and your favorite flavored coffee."

As Tony ate he related the events of the past two days. He couldn't help but notice her face darkening. Despite her noticeable concern, he couldn't contain his happiness and enthusiasm. Occasionally she forced a smile, but it was obvious she was becoming more distressed the longer he talked. Tony decided to force the issue.

"Please, Mama," he begged, "if you don't want me working for Good Shepherd, tell me why."

"What makes you think I don't want you to go there? Did I ever say that? It just makes me sad to think that you'll be leaving us again so soon. I don't see why you can't just go to work for Mr. Lawrence right away. I still don't understand even though you've explained it to me. I'm happy for you, but I will also miss you. I think all mothers feel this way when they realize they have to let their children go."

She walked over to the table and gave him an extra exuberant hug.

"Looks like another 'end of discussion' about the past," Tony thought as he returned her hug with a few kisses thrown in for good measure.

Mama wiped her eyes. "We'd better get your clothes packed so you can be on your way," she said as she turned to leave the room. "I'm truly happy for you; I know you'll be the best employee they ever had. Just promise me you'll stay out of Family matters." She turned and headed for the bedroom before he could respond.

Tony sat there, stunned by her parting words. He had no idea what she had meant. Then he shrugged his shoulders, went to the phone and dialed a familiar number.

"Stroud-Lawrence Funeral Home, Judi Lawrence speaking," a pleasant voice announced.

"Hi Judi, this is Tony."

"Tony!" she said excitedly. "Sorry we didn't get to congratulate you in person. Don had to get back to meet with a family, and then he was master of ceremonies for the retirement party for David Griffiths, our attorney."

"No problem," Tony assured her. "I'm fairly familiar with your high octane lifestyle. The important thing was that you both were able to be there. It meant a lot to me."

"I assume you're in town. Can you come over so we can congratulate you in person? Don has a little something for you."

"Sorry," Tony apologized, "but I only have a few minutes. Is Don there? I have a question to ask him."

"He's out mowing the lawn, and you know how intense he gets when he pretends he's drag racing at Norwalk Speedway. Can't you stop by on your way? He won't mind stopping in mid-race for you."

"O.K., I'll be right over." Tony hung up and headed for the bedroom. He knew it was futile to pose any more questions. He gave Mama a hug goodbye and looked around his room.

"I know I'll be busy for the next few weeks, but I'll call you when I get a break. After all, it's only about fifteen miles from here." He picked up his suitcase, along with several hangers, holding his only suit, four shirts and two pairs of slacks. "Quite an impressive wardrobe for Good Shepherd," he thought.

Mama looked pale as he kissed her on the cheek and headed for the door. She never uttered another word. She just stood there. Now he was really puzzled. With a sense of helplessness, he turned away from her. But he couldn't resist giving it one more try.

"Mama, what did you mean about staying out of Family matters?"

She answered, "Nothing to be concerned about. I'm sorry I mentioned it. Just do your job and come back to us safe and sound."

Tony could have sworn he heard soft sobbing as he left the room. Grudgingly, he backed out of the drive, headed down South Street and turned onto South Franklin. It was only two blocks to the funeral home.

As he approached Stroud-Lawrence Funeral Home, his second home, he couldn't help but look at the magnificent building with a sense of pride. The two-story red brick Italianate house, complimented by its immaculate landscaping, was arguably the most impressive building in the Village. Tony pulled into the drive, got out and pretended to wave a checkered flag in the direction of the approaching mower turned dragster. Don stepped out triumphantly.

"Congratulations and welcome home. Did you land a job yet?" asked Don as he gave him a big hug.

"Yes, as a matter of fact," responded Tony. "That's what I wanted to talk to you about."

"Just remember what I said about taking permanent employment," cautioned Don laughingly.

"I've been offered an apprenticeship at Good Shepherd and signed a contract this morning."

The smile on Don's face evaporated and his voice immediately lost its buoyancy. "What do you know about them?" he asked.

"Not much, just talk at school. They have a great reputation, don't they?"

Don regained his composure. "Yes they do. You could do a lot worse. I'm happy for you."

Tony knew Don too well not to recognize his response was less than enthusiastic.

"What's the matter, Don? Did I make a bad decision? I was going to call you last night, but I was so beat that I fell asleep right in the chair. I had to give them my answer this morning. I'm sorry, because I really wanted your input before I accepted the job."

"You did fine, Tony. You'll be so busy those two years will be a blur," Don answered. "It's such an awesome place I'm afraid you might not want to come back to little old Shaggy Falls."

"Don't worry about that. You and Judi have been so great I can't imagine wanting to work anyplace else."

The two men shook hands, and Tony turned to go to the car.

"Just a minute. I have something for you." Don reached into his shirt pocket and handed Tony an envelope.

"Thanks a million, but you shouldn't have. You've been more than generous to me already."

"Nonsense," countered Don. "Just do us a favor and get rid of that ugly suit. We could put up with it here, but they'll probably laugh you right out of a high-class place like Good Shepherd. Keep in touch," he said as he hopped back on the mower and began revving up the engine.

Tony pulled out, heading for a job that had him more than a little apprehensive.

"I sure hope I'm doing the right thing," he murmured aloud.

5

For the next several days, Tony felt like he was going through final exam week again. "I never believed that this business could involve so much detail and preparation," marveled Tony. "Now I know why apprenticeship is mandatory." He realized that, because of its unique construction, it was actually four individual funeral homes. The business office was an extremely busy place. Efficiency in all aspects of the operation was mandatory in this highly successful business. Attention to detail was almost beyond comprehension. "I can learn so much here if I don't have a nervous breakdown first," sighed Tony.

Since he was being exposed to the internal workings of a large, complex funeral home, Tony's days were extremely busy. Each evening he arrived at his apartment with barely enough energy to crawl into bed. Near the end of the second week, the frantic pace slowed down. The feeling of being totally overwhelmed was beginning to fade. There had been little time for socializing, which was fortunate, because most employees seemed distant and uninterested in him. Everyone seemed to be following his own agenda. This was not exactly what he characterized as "family". Maybe it was his fault since it was not his nature to go out of his way to initiate conversation. This was a skill he definitely needed to enhance. Right now he was barely able to keep pace with his hectic schedule. Refinement of his people skills would come when his days became less of a blur.

⸻≫-◦-≪⸻

One evening late into his second week Tony sat eating dinner. He was totally absorbed in his supper. A voice brought him out of his contemplation of mashed potatoes.

"You should be seeing some light at the end of the tunnel by now." The voice was not familiar, and Tony looked up to see a tall young man about his age. He had seen him periodically but had never been formally introduced.

"Hi, Tony, I'm Pete Boggio, and I was feeling exactly like you about a year ago," said the young man cheerfully. Pete, an apprentice like himself, was the first congenial voice he'd heard among staff members. He had a face that radiated warmth. With his red hair and ruddy complexion, he gave the appearance of someone who thoroughly enjoyed life.

Tony stood and extended his hand. "Nice to meet you, Pete. I was beginning to think that no one was allowed to speak except to issue orders and give instructions." He was overjoyed to be finally talking to someone casually. True to form, though, he did not display it outwardly.

"We are instructed not to provide any unnecessary distractions. You would have enough to do just learning what's going on around here," said Pete. "We needed to give you breathing room. Let me be the first to congratulate you. We should celebrate now that you're back among the living."

Tony smiled and felt relaxed for the first time since arriving at Good Shepherd. "I'd like that very much," said Tony. "Where should we go?"

"Come over to my apartment. We can kick off our shoes and relax over a cold beer or two," said Pete.

"That sounds great," said Tony enthusiastically. "I was about to go off the deep end."

"I know exactly how you feel. It wasn't too long ago that I was in the same boat. Let's go over to my pad and start some serious R & R."

Pete's apartment was directly across the parking lot from Tony's. He had been with Good Shepherd for almost a year after graduating from the University of

Cincinnati's mortuary school. Like Tony, Pete had no inkling why he was selected for an interview, and he, too, had been overwhelmed by their offer.

"I can't figure it out," he mused, "and I'm only half Italian. I'm not sure what the other half is, but it's definitely not Italian." They both laughed. Pete looked more like he belonged behind the bar in an Irish pub.

Occasionally during the evening Tony thought he detected a faint trace of anxiety in Pete's voice as he related certain events that had occurred. A few times he started to say something but stopped short. His caution was understandable to an extent since the two of them had just met.

Pete's sense of humor and general attitude made Tony feel relaxed and glad to have this new friend. He was finally beginning to feel at home. He sensed Pete and he could become close friends. It was hard not to instantly like a person with Pete's infectious personality. Tony found himself envying his easy manner. "He makes me feel like the most important person he's met all day. Sure wish I had that gift," thought Tony.

They talked about everything under the sun for the next two hours. Their general "getting-to-know-you" session obviously had a great therapeutic effect on both men. It appeared Pete had had very little social interaction with anyone on staff. He was pleased to finally have met someone with whom he felt comfortable. Though they were quite different personalities, each detected traits in the other that were admirable. The time literally flew by before they realized they had gone well beyond their normal bedtime. Still, it felt good to just sit and relax. Finally Tony, true to form, spoke.

"I'm sure they'll have a full day planned for us. We'd better hit the sack. Thanks for the drink and the conversation, Pete; next time it's my treat," said Tony. "Maybe we can visit a local bar. I haven't seen an unembalmed female since I arrived."

"And you won't," said Pete. "It's no accident. They

don't employ females. I suppose they have their reasons, but I'm surprised no one has challenged their hiring practices. They seem to be able to do things pretty much their own way. I guess it's not a good idea to challenge them," cautioned Pete. "That's not the only thing around here that borders on bizarre."

Tony looked confused. "What do you mean by that?"

"You need to see for yourself and then decide what you think," explained Pete. "Maybe my imagination is just too active. I really don't want to say anything else that might prejudice you. Actually, this is a great place to prepare you for the future. We're lucky to be here. I've heard we can almost write our own ticket if we leave here with a good recommendation."

His quick change in attitude baffled Tony even more, but he sensed further discussions on the subject were over. He rose, shook Pete's hand and left. Again, apprehensions had clouded an otherwise enjoyable evening. As Tony walked back across the lot to his apartment, he glanced at the main house. A drape quickly closed in one of the upstairs rooms.

Tony and Peter were assigned to pick up a body at Cleveland Hopkins Airport that was arriving from San Francisco after seven a.m. Calling hours had been set for seven o'clock that evening so they decided to leave early to give themselves plenty of time to get back.

A light was on in Bonitto's office. Otherwise there was no evidence of activity. The sun was just beginning to send shafts of light through the trees as they left the grounds. Peter was driving, but he was not his usual lively self.

"I hope this trip will give us a chance to continue last night's discussion," thought Tony. "Things just don't seem quite as right as they should be. Maybe he'll open up more today."

They drove to University Circle and then to Martin Luther King Boulevard. Traffic was sparse and they soon entered the Shoreway. Heading downtown, the Cleveland skyline was now glowing in the early morning sunlight. So far Peter had hardly spoken.

Tony couldn't stand it any longer. "Do you only talk after a few beers? I was hoping to get to know you better and to learn a little more about the business."

"I'm sorry," apologized Pete, "it's not the company. I'm afraid I might have given you the wrong impression. Fact is I'm very happy working at Good Shepherd - there's no problem. My girlfriend and I had a bit of a disagreement recently, and it's been getting me down. She doesn't like the crazy hours and the unpredictable schedule. I keep trying to tell her it's only temporary. I can't bring myself to tell her it's always going to be like this. She'd probably drop me like a hot potato if she knew the truth."

"She's going to find out sooner or later," cautioned Tony.

Pete agreed. "Yeah, but by the time she catches on, I'll be rich and she won't be able to resist me or the big bucks."

They both laughed.

Pete was back to his old self. The only thing that seemed peculiar to Tony was that no more was said about the "questionable" activities at Good Shepherd. Using girlfriend problems as an excuse did not totally satisfy Tony. He had detected a much deeper reason, and that it was somehow related to Good Shepherd. Though he wanted Pete to open up more, he decided to bide his time.

They had reached Dead Man's Curve and were entering the Innerbelt.

"Do you follow the Tribe?" asked Tony.

"I thought everyone did nowadays. Have you been to 'The Jake'?"

"Not as much as I'd like. Tickets are pretty hard to get," said Tony.

"Yeah, not like the good old days at Muny Stadium when you could walk up ten minutes before game time," answered Peter. "It's a trade-off that has benefited everyone."

Heading onto the ramp for Interstate 90, they passed Jacobs Field with its toothbrush-like light towers - a jewel nestled in the heart of the city.

"It's a perfect place to watch a ball game. I saw several in '94 before the sellout record began. Uncle Gino and my cousins took Mama and me to a Fourth of July concert put on by the Cleveland Orchestra at The Jake. Fireworks and the whole bit! It was a great evening, but it was so hot we sat in puddles of our own sweat."

"I saw a lot of games that year too. They were just starting to make their move when the strike shut everything down. If it hadn't been for The Jake, fans would not have forgiven so easily. Nowadays it reminds me of one of Yogi Berra's famous remarks."

"You mean the one where he says, 'The place is so crowded nobody ever goes there anymore'?"

They both laughed. They were on Interstate 90 crossing the bridge over the Cuyahoga River.

"Did I tell you I grew up on the West Side?" asked Peter.

"No, but you didn't have to. I could tell from your accent. You guys from the wrong side of the River all talk funny." Again they were laughing. A strong bond was developing between the two men. In many aspects they were quite dissimilar. Tony's more reticent nature was complemented by Pete's outgoing demeanor. It was a good mix, and Tony found himself becoming comfortable with him.

Though he would still take his work seriously, he felt he would now find it easier to unwind when the situation warranted. Pete was definitely good medicine for the stoic Tony. In many ways Peter reminded him of his old friend and mentor back in Chagrin Falls.

They continued driving on 71, past Metro General Curve and the Metropark Zoo. As they were nearing West 150th Street Exit, Peter remarked, "Here's the exit to my home. I've lived in West Park my whole life. I was born in Fairview General Hospital. After my parents passed away, I inherited the house. When I'm finished at Good Shepherd, I plan on getting a job with a funeral home near there."

"At least you were close to the airport. When did your parents die?" asked Tony.

"When I was in college. They were out late one night in the winter. A drunk driver hit them head on. Both of them were killed instantly," replied Pete.

"That's really tough. But at least you knew them. My dad died when I was little. I don't even remember him," responded Tony.

"My dad was really a great guy. I wish he were here now. He had a knack for listening to me, and without saying much, helping me figure out what to do when I was in a bind," Peter said.

They reached the cargo area at Hopkins International Airport and quickly loaded their "passenger" in the hearse. Back on the freeway, they were beginning to feel the effects of rush hour traffic, but as yet it hadn't peaked.

"Once we get through Cleveland most of the traffic will be going the other way," said Peter. "We should get back with hours to spare."

"They'll have plenty of time to get our passenger looking just right before the seven o'clock calling hours," agreed Tony.

Once more on the Innerbelt heading the opposite direction, Tony remarked, "I've been to the Rock 'n' Roll Hall of Fame twice. Once with my cousins, and once with a date. The architecture is really neat. It's worth driving by just to look at it."

"I've only been there once. But I liked the Elvis exhibit the best. And I've been to the Great Lakes Science Museum next door three times. I saw the whale movie in the Omnimax Theatre. Now that was really cool, leaning back in the chair and seeing the movie all around you," Pete said enthusiastically.

"When we went to the Hall of Fame, we took the rapid transit from Green Road all the way down to it. It's almost like a ride at Cedar Point! Cleveland has really come a long way since the days of the Burning River," exclaimed Tony.

They turned onto Martin Luther King Drive, and continued past the Cultural Gardens.

"This is one of the prettiest drives in Cleveland. And this is probably the prettiest time of the year," said Peter. "It always makes me think of the Art Museum with all the statues mixed in with the flowers."

"It makes me think of the Botanical Gardens," countered Tony. "That used to be one of Mama's favorite places to go at Christmas. But I always liked it best in the summer. All those flowers, plants and trees strategically placed - it looked like an English garden."

The sun was high and boring in on them as they reached Good Shepherd.

"Let's get a cup of coffee," said Tony. "I feel like I've already been up for hours."

"Guess what!" said Peter as he pushed him through the door of the small cafeteria. "We have!"

———————

"I've got a great idea," chirped Peter. "You said you once lived in Little Italy when you were very young. Have you been back since?"

"I know you'll find it hard to believe, but I've never set foot there."

"Well," responded Peter. "I'd say it's high time you did. It's a fascinating place. I love to go there on the rare occasions when I can squeeze out a little free time. I'll tell you what - next time it looks like we're going to have a few hours to ourselves, we'll have lunch or supper at one of their many great restaurants. Hopefully we'll also have time to walk around a little. You can go back to your roots."

"Sounds good to me," agreed Tony as they separated to attend to their assignments for that day.

Tony couldn't get Peter's invitation off his mind. No one in his family had ever suggested "going back home." This, among other things, had always puzzled him since it was so accessible to Chagrin Falls. It was almost as if that page of his life story had been torn from the book. It was just one of the many questions he had harbored. The thought of going back made him a bit anxious, though he couldn't have said why. Old memories began resurfacing for the rest of the day. Maybe he'd meet someone who knew his father. Maybe he'd finally learn what had happened to him. Maybe he'd learn what had been kept from him his entire life.

"Maybe, maybe, maybe," he thought. "It's nothing but wishful thinking. What am I going to do - carry around a sign saying, 'Hey, I'm Tony Amico. I used to live here. Did you know my dad? Do I look like him? What did he do for a living? Was he a good man?' That'll really get me some answers, I bet!"

A look of longing and sadness clouded his face as a tear appeared. He quickly brushed it away while casually glancing around to see if anyone had noticed. No matter how hard he tried, it was impossible to dismiss the feeling of melancholy that engulfed him.

7

A few days later, as luck would have it, Peter announced, "Get ready buddy, today we're going to visit Little Italy."

Tony could feel the electricity surging through him. Trying to conceal his excitement, he exclaimed, "Good, I haven't had decent Italian food since I left home." His pulse quickened, and he felt his face getting hot. A voice within blared, "Let's go for it." Though he always tried to appear under control, his hands were shaking with anticipation.

Stopping at the gate, they were greeted by Stan, the guard at the Gate House. His smiling face and pleasant demeanor were perfectly suited for his position since he was the first person visitors to Good Shepherd encountered. When they announced their destination, Stan's eyes lit up as he exclaimed, "Why don't you stop at Mama Santa's? My niece works the lunch shift. She'll give you special attention. I'll call her right now and tell her to expect you."

"That sounds like a winner," said Peter. "I sure hope she doesn't look like you."

"Very funny. You should be so lucky. She wouldn't even bat an eye at the likes of you two. Besides, she's married and has five kids."

"Great," said Tony, "then we're both safe." They pulled out and headed for Murray Hill.

———⟫•◦•⟪———

Stan picked up the phone and punched the intercom connecting him to Bonitto's office.

"Yes, Stan, what is it?"

"Just reporting, like you asked, Mr. Bonitto. Peter

and Tony are going to Little Italy for lunch at Mama Santa's."

"Thank you, Stan. I appreciate the information." With that, he hung up and quickly dialed another number.

────◆────

As Peter drove along, Tony's body was occupying space in the car, but his mind was in another dimension. Scenes flashed past the window, but there was no recognition. Suddenly Peter's voice snapped him back to reality.

"We'll park here at the East end so we can walk the length of the business section."

It was a beautiful late spring day and the street was bustling with activity. Tony felt a strange kinship as he absorbed the scene. He was flooded with good vibrations as his eyes scoured every nook and cranny.

It was clear the area had gone through a severe decline caused by the flight of younger people to the suburbs. One by one the shops along Mayfield Road had disappeared, as had the Mayfield Theater sometime earlier. By the late seventies Murray Hill Elementary School closed its doors for good.

As they walked along the busy sidewalk, evidence of the Renaissance justified the steadfast faith of its residents. The numerous galleries now occupying the old shops joined the restaurants that had remained popular. The delicious aromas of fresh baked goods from Corbo's and Presti's famous bakeries tempted their appetites.

Choosing a restaurant was a difficult task. Primo Vino, Guarino's, Mama Santa's, Porcelli's, Tratorria Roman Gardens - each had its own special attraction. Finally they decided to return to Mama Santa's on the advice of Stan. After all, they didn't want to disappoint his niece.

"Maybe some night we can bring dates to the Baricelli Inn," said Pete.

"That's bound to impress them. I hope we'll still have time today to go over to the old school. You'll be amazed at what's been done there. The new part was converted into condominiums. In the school's older section shops and offices replaced the classrooms. Wait till you see the Riley Hawk Gallery that is in the old auditorium. Artists producing some of the world's finest creations in glass are featured there."

"Sounds like a visit to Little Italy is a treat for all the senses," said Tony. "Let's eat."

They crossed the busy street and approached Mama Santa's.

"Here we are," announced Peter. "I've eaten here before - the food is excellent. You've been unusually quiet. Is anything wrong?"

"No, but I have the strangest feeling. This is a visit that's long overdue."

Though the streets were quite busy, it was still early. The lunch crowd had not yet arrived so the restaurant was virtually deserted. As the door closed, the light and sounds of the street vanished. Silence engulfed them as their eyes slowly adjusted to the dimly lit entrance. A young woman approached carrying menus and greeted them by name. Their eyes widened in surprise by the recognition.

"Please follow me, gentlemen." They passed through the main dining area and entered a smaller adjacent room. They were led to a table on the far side of the room. She placed a menu in front of the seat against the wall and held the chair for Tony as Pete sat down opposite him. Once they were seated, she announced, "Your waitress will be here in a moment. Please enjoy your meal."

Before they could respond, she disappeared into the shadows. Pete and Tony looked at one another, wondering what other surprises were in store.

Presently an older woman appeared. She greeted them cheerfully. "Welcome, Mr. Amico and Mr. Boggio. My name is Lena, and I will be your server." Her demeanor instantly put them at ease.

"How did you know our names?" asked Peter.

"Uncle Stan called and told me you might be coming in for lunch," she explained. "He described you perfectly."

"I'm not even going to touch that one," laughed Peter.

They each ordered a tall glass of draft beer. They were just picking up their menus when an elderly man entered the room followed by two younger men. The hostess had not accompanied them. They approached a table on the opposite side of the room. One of the younger men held a chair for the older man as he slowly eased into a position facing Tony. The man raised his head and their eyes locked. Although the room was dimly lit, the old man's features were quite clear. Tony studied him carefully, almost hypnotized by his gaze. His dark eyes were partially obscured by bushy white eyebrows. A heavy shock of coarse, white hair dominated his features. He looked like a kindly grandfather. A strange feeling came over Tony as he struggled to look away.

A man in a business suit appeared with a bottle of wine and a solitary glass. He poured out a small portion, and his elderly guest slowly raised the glass to his lips. An approving nod assured the man it was to his liking. He proceeded to fill the glass, gave a slight bow and backed out of the room. During the entire time, the old man's eyes never strayed from Tony. The old man picked up his glass of wine and raised it in a toast to him before taking another sip.

The appearance of the waitress distracted Tony, breaking the spell. Shortly after ordering, he returned his attention to the old man. To his surprise, the table was empty. There was no trace of the old man's presence.

Peter noted the confusion on Tony's face. "What's wrong? You look like you've seen a ghost."

"Did you happen to notice the people who came in a short time ago?"

"Yeah, I noticed, but really didn't pay much attention. Why?"

"There was this old man. I mean really old. He just kept staring at me. It was the strangest feeling - like I knew him from somewhere. It seemed he knew me too. I had to fight the compulsion to get up and walk over to him. The next time I looked, he was gone. It was really weird."

"Sorry, pal, I can't help you. Maybe he just looked like somebody else you know."

Just then the waitress appeared with their food.

"Excuse me, Lena," said Tony. "Did you happen to notice the people who were sitting at the other table?"

"There was no one seated there while I was in the room, but I can ask the hostess if you'd like."

"Maybe you could ask the guy that was dressed in a suit. He brought them some wine," said Tony, almost pleadingly.

"There's no one working here that wears a suit. In fact, the only male working is the noon cook. Do you want me to ask him?"

Totally frustrated, Tony snapped back in an uncharacteristic fashion. "I don't understand how someone can walk in here, be served a drink by another guy and no one sees them. Don't you think that's a little strange?"

"I'm sorry, sir, I . . ."

"That's all right, Lena, it's not your fault. I'm the one who should apologize."

Peter was confused by Tony's outburst. He studied his friend as he picked at his food. It was obvious that the excitement of earlier in the day had evaporated.

Hoping to take the edge off Tony's frayed nerves and not wishing to make matters worse, Peter tried to change the subject. "Let's make a little detour on the way back. Have you ever seen Rodin's statue of 'The Thinker' at the Art Museum? It's his original. Back around 1972 someone blew a hole in the base of the statue with a bomb. It's been left there as a memorial."

Tony gave an unenthusiastic nod and continued picking at his food. He could not erase the image of the old man's gaze. "Who was he? Where did he come from and where did he go?" He was positive it wasn't a coincidence, but what was the significance of this bizarre scenario?

As they entered the car, Tony finally broke the silence. "Peter, if you don't mind I'd rather just head back. This day has suddenly gone sour, and I can't explain why. I just know that was not a figment of my imagination. That old man definitely knew me."

"It's okay with me. But next time, let's go to one of the special exhibits at the Art Museum. I really miss not going once in awhile. What's the point of living in a city with a world-class art museum if you never go to it?" Peter asked.

Tony answered, "Next time. I'm just not interested in doing anything else today. I promise I'll even go to the Crawford Auto Museum with you if you want.'

Peter seemed satisfied, but the return trip was shrouded in silence. For one of the few times in his life, Peter could not come up with the appropriate words.

Tony and Peter left their apartments at exactly the same time and were surprised to see an unusual amount of activity in the parking lot below. Employees were busy washing and polishing every available vehicle. This was atypical because washing would suffice at normal funerals. This had to be someone special.

Unable to resist, Peter yelled down to a young man furiously polishing the hood of a black limousine. "What's going on? I've never seen you work this hard. Who died - Mayor White?"

"Some rich dude. I think his name was Braxton or Blockston."

"Wow!" exclaimed Peter as he rushed toward Tony. "No wonder they're working like crazy. If it's who I think it is, calling Claymore Broxton merely rich is like saying the Pope is sort of religious."

"Yes," responded Tony. "Even I've heard of him. We've definitely got a big day ahead of us."

They hurried over to the office to receive their assignments. The funeral was to be held at the Masonic Auditorium to accommodate the anticipated crowd of mourners. Tony and Peter were to go directly to the Wade Chapel at Lake View Cemetery to stand guard until the family arrived for private services and burial.

Tony was excited. He'd heard so much about the cemetery, one of the oldest and largest in Cleveland, but had never had the opportunity to visit the final resting-place of the rich and famous. Peter was familiar with the grounds and its celebrities so he volunteered to give Tony a quick tour before they were to assume their duties.

Entering the prestigious cemetery was like opening

the pages of a history book. It had been founded when America was less than 100 years old, and many of Cleveland's famous people were buried there. Significant contributors were immortalized in stone, sculpture and statuary. This, combined with beautiful landscaping, made a visit to Lake View Cemetery a truly memorable experience.

Tony was immediately impressed as they pulled through the stone gates at the south end just off Mayfield Road.

"I'll give you a quick tour on our way down to the Wade Chapel. There's too much to see now. We can always come back," said Peter.

"Lead on, mister tour guide," said Tony excitedly.

They turned left and followed the curving drive. Tony strained to read the inscriptions on the headstones as they made their way toward the Garfield Memorial, the largest, most impressive structure in Lake View, befitting the cemetery's most famous inhabitant.

"We can't take time to go in now," said Peter. "We'll want to come back when we can give it a well-deserved inspection. I understand President and Mrs. Garfield's caskets are always visible in their crypt. He is the only American president displayed like that."

"Very illuminating. Let's go. I can't wait for our next stop."

They circled in front of the massive sandstone building and spiraled down to the next main drive. Directly across towered the John D. Rockefeller memorial.

"The carvings were done by a fellow countryman, Joseph Carabelli. He was one of Little Italy's earliest settlers. He founded a company that still exists."

"Wow, you're just a font of knowledge," said Tony. "I think you missed your calling."

"That's only the tip of the iceberg. Take any one of these drives, and you'll see famous inventors, educators, politicians, industrialists, statesmen, musicians and philanthropists."

"I can see you've done your homework," said Tony. "If you could spend some time with any person here, who would you choose?"

Peter thought for a moment and then replied hesitantly, "I'd like to talk to Elliott Ness."

Tony began to laugh until he noticed the unusually serious look on his face. "Why in the world would it be 'Mr. Untouchable'?"

Peter's voice lost its usual buoyancy. "I'd like to get some advice. There are problems that are getting beyond my ability to cope." Suddenly the excitement and anticipation of the day evaporated.

Tony was mesmerized as Peter continued. "There are things going on that are really getting to me. I know you've noticed, and I appreciate the fact you haven't pushed for answers. But for now it will have to remain that way. I'm sorry I even brought it up. Forget what I said. Let's go to work."

"How can I possibly forget what he said?" thought Tony. "O.K. pal, it's your call. Just remember I'll always be available to aid a goomba in distress."

"Thanks, Tony, I already knew that. Hopefully, the request won't be necessary."

Silence took command as they approached the Wade Chapel. Each man's thoughts precluded any further exchange. They performed their duties the rest of the day under a cloud of unanswered questions.

It was Friday afternoon before Tony finally had a chance to sit down and relax. The past five days were the kind he remembered would cause Don to get just a touch "short" with his employees back at Stroud-Lawrence. He had been on the go fourteen to sixteen hours a day all week. It was a toss-up whether he would finish this week's issue of the *Chagrin Valley Times* or fall sound asleep.

He was just starting to delve into Barry Goodrich's column when he heard a loud rap at his door. Startled, he nearly fell out of his chair.

In burst Pete. "I'm glad you're sitting down," he shouted excitedly. "What I'm about to tell you would have knocked you right on your keister."

Tony's eyes were wide open as he braced himself to hear bad news. "What is it this time? My mind and body are so numb, the only thing that would make me hurt more than I do now is another pickup at the county morgue."

"My, aren't we the negative one today," mocked Pete. "Well, Mister Gloom and Doom, I'm here to tell you we have the whole weekend off."

Tony rolled onto the floor and started kicking his feet in the air as fast as they would go. "I don't believe it," he screamed. "You can't be serious! They're really letting us out?"

"It's on the level. Apparently, the Scarlettos have a baptism and two communions this weekend. Family members are coming in from all over the country. They're actually shutting Good Shepherd down for the entire weekend. You should have seen Bonitto. I think it hurt

him to tell us. I don't think the man would smile if he hit
the lotto. I'm still in shock. I can't even think of what to
do. I feel like the guy who was released from the peniten-
tiary after spending fifty years behind bars. He was so
confused in the outside world, he begged them to let him
back in."

"Well, I've got an idea," exclaimed Tony. "Since
they're shutting down operations, we don't have to stay
here, do we?"

"No way," said Pete. "We're outta here. What's your
plan?"

"How'd you like to spend the weekend in beautiful
Chagrin Falls?"

"Any place is better than this, even Shaggy Falls,"
teased Pete.

"I was just reading the local paper, and this happens
to be the best weekend of the entire year - Blossom Time!"

"Blossom Time? Now that really sounds exciting.
I've been so busy I didn't even notice there were blossoms.
I guess it's got to beat staying here."

"Just wait. I guarantee you'll eat those words. My
hometown knows how to party. The local Jaycees have
created a weekend that is nonstop. If you don't have a
great time, I'll do all your 'certified' runs to City Hall for
a month."

"Now you've got my interest. Let's pack and get out
of here."

"I'll pick you up in ten minutes. If you're not ready,
I'm leaving without you," announced Tony in mock seriousness.

Pete was bounding down the steps before he could
say another word. Tony figured he'd just surprise Mama.
She'd be so happy to see him; bringing Pete would be an
added bonus.

"It's been so busy here I really haven't thought much
about home," he mused. He could feel the excitement
surging as he anticipated the reunion with his family. "I
really do miss them. I wish my time here were over so I

could get back to where I belong." In spite of everything Good Shepherd had to offer, his heart and loyalties were firmly entrenched.

⟺⟐⟐⟐⟸

As Tony backed out of the garage, Pete was already pounding on the window. He jumped in and held an envelope in front of Tony's face. "Here, put ten bucks in this."

"What's that for?"

"First guy that says one word about Good Shepherd loses ten bucks."

"That's a deal," said Tony. "My lips are sealed. You might as well give me your ten spot now."

It was only about a thirty-minute drive, but to Tony it seemed to be taking an eternity. He was anxious to show his new friend the town of which he was so proud. Finally they reached the top of Grove Hill, and there before them was a panoramic view of the Village. It was late afternoon, and there was activity everywhere. Tony paused at the crest to allow Pete time to absorb the entire scene.

"Welcome to Chagrin Falls and Blossom Time." Tony had purposely taken this route to give Pete the full effect. The view from the top of Grove Hill was, without a doubt, the most impressive way to introduce a newcomer.

"Wow!" exclaimed Pete. "Now I'm beginning to see why you talk about this place so much. Are you sure this isn't like the village of Brigadoon? How could I have missed it?"

"I can't believe you've never been here, if only to go to the Popcorn Shop and stop at the Falls. Seems like everyone has done that, even 'foreigners' from the West Side like you."

"I guess I've led a pretty sheltered life on the other side of the River, but that's all going to change after a wild Blossom Time weekend. Think you can fix me up with the queen of Blossom Time?" kidded Pete.

"She's just a senior in high school, you jerk, but we'll go to the alumni party at the Township Hall and see what happens. First, let's head for home so you can meet the family."

Tony was proud of his hometown. He was even more proud of his family. To him they were the salt of the earth- hard working and honest. Uncle Gino had labored as a landscaper all his life and was now foreman of a large crew at Hemlock Landscaping. His cousins were also very popular. As they walked through town nearly everyone greeted them. Tony was impressed by the respect shown his cousins. He would tease them saying, "When Mayor Champlin retires, one of you should throw your hat in the ring. Either one of you would win in a landslide."

Peter and Tony made their way down Grove Hill and slowly drove through the busy business section.

"I see four traffic lights on the main drag. Do they turn to caution lights after dark when they roll up the sidewalks?"

"No, wise guy, and we have several more traffic lights in town. If you don't show a little respect, I won't let you see them." Occasionally someone would yell his name, and Tony would return his greeting with a wave. As they crossed the Main Street Bridge, folks were just beginning to enter the carnival at Riverside Park.

They turned off Main Street at Triangle Park and headed south on Franklin Street. After a short distance, Tony proudly announced, "There's my second home on the left." A large sign with gold letters identified the Stroud-Lawrence Funeral Home.

"Very impressive. It's exactly the way I would have imagined it. Someday your name will be added to that fancy sign."

"No way," said Tony, though he craved that more than anything in the world.

Don and Judi Lawrence were just heading down the driveway. They often walked to and from work since their home was only a block away on Walnut Street. Tony honked the horn and pulled in. Their faces lit up as soon as they recognized the driver.

"Don't tell me they fired you already," teased Don.

"No, as a matter of fact, we've done so well they gave us the weekend off as a reward."

"And they couldn't have picked a better weekend to do it," said Judi.

"This is my friend, Pete Boggio. He's already put in a year of apprenticeship at Good Shepherd - and lived to tell about it."

"It's nice to meet you at last," said Pete. "Tony has told me so much about you."

"Was he complimentary, or did he tell the truth?"

"Pay no attention to him. He thinks he's a comedian," laughed Judi. "He's not always like this, Pete. Most of the time, he's worse."

"Hey, our Friday night supper club is dining at the Eagles. Why don't you join us? Afterwards we can get into a hot game of euchre."

Judi interrupted, "Don, you're talking to a couple of young men with active hormones. Don't you think they might have something more exciting planned than an evening at the Eagles? Especially this weekend?"

Tony and Pete just grinned.

"I'm sure we'll see you both later this weekend, but right now we've got to get home so Pete can meet the family," said Tony.

"Pete, I want to alert you that Tony gets wild and crazy just once a year, and it happens to be Blossom Time weekend," warned Don, tongue in cheek. "I hope you know how to talk your way out of fights."

"Very funny, Don. They have to assign one off-duty policeman just to shadow me," quipped Tony.

They all laughed as Tony circled around to the back of the parking lot and pulled out onto Franklin Street.

"What's that gigantic tent doing in the parking lot of the funeral home?" asked Pete.

"They have a huge party after the parade on Sunday. It's become quite a tradition. Too bad we have to miss it. Half the town shows up."

"Yeah," sighed Pete. "Back to reality at Good Shepherd Sweatshop."

"Thanks, Pete."

"For what?"

"You just lost ten bucks."

"You set me up for that, didn't you?"

Tony just laughed as he grabbed the envelope out of Pete's shirt pocket.

Tony pulled into the driveway on South Street. The house was strangely quiet, and there was no car in the drive. Momentarily puzzled, Tony slapped his forehead.

"Oh, I just remembered. They were all going away this weekend."

"They must not share your affection for good ole Blossom Time."

"Actually they do, but Uncle Gino always attends the reunion of his old army outfit. This year it's in Nashville so they went on a mini vacation. I guess we have to rough it. Too bad - Mama's a fantastic cook. We'll walk up town for supper. The traffic is crazy so you have to be really lucky to get a parking place closer anyway."

They quickly unloaded their suitcases. Full of anticipation, they were walking up South Franklin when they heard a loud swooshing sound. Pete jumped a foot in the air as Tony howled with delight. They heard it again, only closer. Tony pointed up to the sky as a multicolored hot air balloon skimmed the treetops at the rear of the funeral home parking lot. The sunlight reflected off its surface as it silently glided past. Another appeared, even more colorful than the last. Then another and another.

For the next fifteen or twenty minutes they watched the magnificent colorful parade.

"The upper air currents must have been just right. We don't usually see them right overhead in the Village."

"That's what I call a real show," marveled Pete. "To

tell the truth, I've been eating crow ever since we hit Grove Hill. Your town has captivated me."

"Just an added Blossom Time bonus," said Tony. "The balloons have become quite a tradition in the last several years."

When they were convinced that no more balloons were headed their way, they began walking up the tree-lined street toward town. The spectacular sight had temporarily replaced their need for nourishment.

"We've got some really nice places to eat, but they'll all be busy. We might as well stop at Dink's and take our chances." They crossed the street at the Triangle Park and entered a small, crowded restaurant.

"Dink's! How'd they ever get that name?"

"It's a long story, but I'll give you the short version," said Tony. "The restaurant opened about 1950 in Cleveland Heights. The owner's name was George Mawby, whose nickname happened to be . . ."

"I'll bet it was 'Dink'," interrupted Peter.

"How'd you guess? You must be psychic," mocked Tony. "Anyway, to make a long story short, Sisters Hilda and Gail bought Dink out and moved to Chagrin in 1960. The name stuck, and the rest is history."

"I'm glad you gave me the short version. If it had been any longer, I'd have starved to death. Can we eat now?" begged Peter.

Tony was greeted by a number of people who were also dining. Many of them called him "Little Digger." Few called him by his first name. Pete was amused and seized the opportunity to rag on his friend. He had noted genuine affection in their voices, and he envied this special relationship. He'd never lived in or known this type of close-knit community. Tony, a little embarrassed by this display, started to say something.

"Don't bother to explain, Tony. I think it's really cool. In my humble opinion, you're one lucky dude. I'm sure I can guess the identity of Big Digger."

Tony realized that Pete was developing a real affinity

for this special place.

He announced, "I'll get the check since I suckered you into losing your bet. You get the tip. Then I have another treat for you."

They left Dink's, crossed the Triangle and walked up the other side of the street. Just as they passed a small shop, a voice boomed out from the entrance.

"I guess now that you're a big-time undertaker, you're too snooty to stop in and greet old friends." Both men turned to face Jim Lewis as he stepped out of the doorway of the Fireside Book Shop and extended his hand. Tony grasped it with a hardy shake.

"I'm sorry, Jim. I just assumed you'd be schmoozing at the alumni reunion by now," said Tony.

"I hope you can spare a few precious moments to introduce your friend to a lowly book shop proprietor," complained Jim.

"Peter Boggio, meet Jim Lewis, the owner of the finest book shop in all of Chagrin Falls."

"Nice to meet you, Pete. Obviously Tony neglected to mention it's the only book shop in Chagrin Falls."

"We're heading for the Township Hall. Would you care to join us?" asked Tony.

"Thanks for the invitation. but, in our infinite wisdom, we've scheduled a wine and cheese reception for Les Roberts, Cleveland's most famous author. As if there's not enough going on this weekend," Jim snorted.

They all had a good laugh as Peter and Tony turned to continue on their way.

They headed toward the north end of town. A large crowd was milling around in front of a small shop. Everyone seemed to be either eating ice cream or munching popcorn.

"This is our famous Popcorn Shop overlooking the Falls. I can't believe you've never been here. Almost everyone in Northeastern Ohio knows about it. It's probably the most identifying feature of the Village other than the Falls. We'll stop in here for dessert."

When they had made their selection, Tony directed Pete down the stairs to the Falls. It was twilight as they paused to watch the spectacular scene. It had rained hard the previous evening, which also seemed to be a Blossom Time tradition. The water was roaring over the falls, sending up thin veils of mist that were dancing in the floodlights. Pete paused to take in the awesome sight.

"This town amazes me more by the minute," he declared. "I really have missed out never having been here before."

"I told you that you wouldn't be disappointed."

"Right you are," agreed Pete. "Don't tell me there's more!"

They continued on their way toward the north end of town. Up ahead another crowd was mingling in front of an old, official-looking brick building.

"This is Township Hall. Our high school Alumni Association holds a big reunion here each year on Friday evening during Blossom Time. The place is packed with grads that span fifty or sixty years. It's another of the weekend's highlights, especially for the younger graduates," Tony explained.

Tony acknowledged the greetings of several people as they walked up the rough-hewn stone steps to the entrance. Just inside, tables were set up, and seated around them were several retired teachers. The hall was already packed to capacity.

"Welcome home, Little Digger." The familiar voice belonged to Tom Mattern, Tony's former middle school history teacher, and presently the school's Alumni Director.

"Hi, Mr. Mattern. Looks like you have another hit on your hands," exclaimed Tony. "You've sure added a great dimension to an already fabulous weekend."

"Thanks, Tony, but you have to have a lot of good people helping to pull it off. I'm sure you recognize all these folks sitting here."

Tony did. They had all played some role in his education at Chagrin Falls. There was Mrs. Moore, his third grade teacher, looking as perky as ever. Mrs. Maus and Mrs. Hubbard had not actually taught him, but they were heavily involved in all aspects of school life. Miss Davenport and Mrs. Barker had been teachers in the middle school. Tony proceeded to introduce Pete to everyone.

"Tony, I think you're old enough to call me by my first name, " said Miss Davenport. "After all, there's only a few years age difference."

"Yeah, and I'm the tooth fairy," kidded Mrs. Barker. They all laughed as Tony and Pete entered the hall and merged into the crowd.

After an hour of introductions and small talk, both men began feeling the effects of their grueling week and the long day. They agreed it was time to head home and get a decent night's sleep for a change. As they walked back toward South Street, Pete couldn't help but express his appreciation.

"This was a great idea, Tony. Thanks for bringing me along. I've never had the opportunity to experience anything like this. You probably take it all for granted, but to an outsider, it's like living in a Norman Rockwell painting."

"That's an interesting way of putting it, Pete. I never thought of it that way, but it seems like a pretty accurate description."

The South section of town was quiet in contrast to the throngs milling around just a few blocks north. Muffled sounds of music were all that shattered the solitude. Streetlight filtered through the trees as a steady parade of folks was slowly walking back home. Children carried balloons or stuffed animals, and the adults talked quietly. Everyone was enjoying the pleasant evening.

Occasionally an automobile broke the spell, but otherwise it was like walking down a tree-lined street at the turn of the century. Both men shared a feeling of contentment as they slowly walked, absorbed in the spell it cast.   They turned into the driveway of Tony's home, both regretting that the all-too-brief moment had to end.

10

Within minutes both men were in bed and sound asleep. They had set no alarm and planned to sleep well past their normal wake-up time at Good Shepherd. After all, they were on a mini vacation. Why not take full advantage of an opportunity that might not present itself for quite some time?

A loud sound made Tony bolt upright. It was still quite dark. The room was dimly illuminated as shadows danced in the moonlight. The eerie scene made him feel like he had awakened in the middle of an old black and white horror movie. He gave a quick, uncontrolled shiver as he heard the sound again. There was no mistaking it this time. It came from Pete's room and sounded like high-pitched sobbing. The sound gave him goosebumps. He could feel waves of them coursing uncontrollably over him. As he sat up, he turned on the light. He quietly got out of bed and slowly walked to the door. He was about to reach for the doorknob when the door flew open. A dark figure stood before him. Tony recoiled in terror as the "thing" emitted another bone-chilling sob.

To Tony's relief, the light from his own room exposed the menacing apparition - Pete, apparently still sound asleep. Tony grabbed his friend by the shoulders and began shaking him gently and calling out his name.

Pete's eyes opened wide as he slumped forward. Tony caught him and held him until he could feel the strength returning to Pete's body. They slowly walked over to the bed and sat on the edge. Although he was only in boxer shorts and a T-shirt, Pete was soaked with perspiration.

"What happened, Pete?" he implored. "You scared

me to death."

"I guess I must have had a bad dream," he allowed.

"Bad dream! That's putting it mildly. From the state you were in, I'd rank it pretty high on the nightmare scale."

"I guess I agree with you. It's not the first one I've had lately. I just hope it's the last."

"Can you remember anything? Sometimes it helps to talk about it."

"Not really," he said hesitantly. "I'm sorry I woke you."

Tony knew Pete wasn't volunteering all he knew, but this was not the time to push the issue. "Can I get you anything?"

"No thanks, I'll be fine now. Sorry I disturbed you. I'll stick a sock in my mouth so it won't happen again."

"That's no problem. I'm relieved to know our house isn't haunted. Are you sure there isn't anything you want to talk about?" He knew he was prying, but he was genuinely concerned for his friend.

"I guess I'd just like to try to get back to sleep, but thanks for asking."

As he headed back to his room, Tony could not help but feel there was a great deal more to this "incident" than Pete was willing to divulge.

⟫◦⟪

After a restless night, Tony awoke much earlier than he had planned. He quickly dressed and slipped quietly down the stairs to brew some much-needed coffee. To his surprise, Pete was up and dressed. He was standing in front of the living room window staring out at nothing in particular.

Not wishing to startle him, especially after last night, he went directly to the kitchen where he noisily went about preparing coffee. In spite of the commotion, Pete never budged or acknowledged Tony's presence.

"It's like he's in a trance," thought Tony. Finally he called, "Hey Pete. Are you ready for some coffee?"

After a pause, Pete slowly turned and walked toward him.

"You bet I am. Thought you'd never ask." The tone of his voice seemed to indicate the "old Pete" was back. Tony's concerns lessened as they sat down at the kitchen table.

Hoping he would volunteer to shed some light on his bizarre behavior, Tony began, "You gave me quite a start last night. I hope you're feeling better."

"Thanks, I feel great. Slept like the proverbial log after our little incident."

"Little incident!" thought Tony. "He was terrified. What is he trying to hide?"

Attempting to be casual, Tony said, "That's good to know. I'm not sure my nerves could handle a repeat performance."

"I've been thinking," Pete said. "I left a ton of paperwork back at the sweatshop, and it would be a good time to catch up without the usual interruptions. What do you say we head back this afternoon? I guess I'm not as up to a wild and crazy weekend as I thought."

Tony fought to conceal his disappointment and genuine surprise at Pete's request.

"It's your call, Pete. I had hoped to show you around some more. There will be other times, but it won't be Blossom Time."

"Thanks, Tony. I appreciate it. But you don't have to miss Blossom because of me. I could take the car and come back for you on Sunday if you'd like."

"No, it's fine. We'll leave whenever you say."

Pete was obviously feeling a bit guilty because of his unexpected change of plans.

"Let's make a day of it. I'm sure I haven't seen all that Chagrin Falls has to offer. I'm still waiting to meet some of your old girlfriends, or is that just a myth?"

"I'm afraid it's more fiction than fact. The truth is I

never really had time for all that stuff. School, working for Don and my family seemed to occupy most of my energy."

"Well I guess that's Chagrin Falls female population's loss," kidded Pete. "You'll have plenty of time to make up for lost opportunities when you become a wealthy playboy funeral director."

They both laughed, knowing all too well that leisure time was a luxury they would seldom experience.

"There was one other place I'd like to stop. Then we can head back. My favorite place other than my 'two homes' is the old hardware store just across the bridge. I used to spend what little free time I had getting harassed by the employees."

They finished their coffee. Tony scribbled a note for his family and left it on the kitchen table.

"Actually, Mama would know I was here as soon as she walked into her kitchen. A note wouldn't even be necessary."

They hopped in the car and headed up town. Most Blossom Time activities hadn't yet begun so the main street was relatively uncongested. They pulled in front of a tall building that looked like something out of a Charles Dickens novel.

The Chagrin Hardware and Supply was the oldest continually operating establishment in the Valley. It was and still is the hub of the Village. Each day, especially on Saturday, a wide assortment of folks could be found visiting in the store. They ranged from the "real Chagrinites" to yuppie weekend "do-it-yourselfers", from society matrons visiting from the posh suburbs of greater Cleveland to "cone lickers" (non-Chagrinites) pushing strollers in to buy corn to feed the ducks in adjacent Riverside Park. Talk with "old timers" about "the way it used to be" was not out of the ordinary. A hot topic was always how the local sports teams were faring and what the coach should have done to win the game on Friday night. Where the fish were hitting and who had caught the biggest "lie" was also discussed along with the usual assortment of bad jokes. Chagrin Hardware was truly a unique place and one of Chagrin Falls' treasures.

As they walked in the door, Pete was almost scalped by the life-size Indian brave blocking his path. A voice from the rear of the store announced to everyone, but no one in particular, "Oh, oh, here comes Little Digger. Watch out - if he gets close to you, he'll take his tape out and start measuring you up."

"I forgot to tell you, Pete, this is a family-owned establishment," Tony announced in an equally loud voice. "They are all a little weird, but harmless. This is Jack, a Don Rickles wannabe. He keeps us all humble."

Susie, who possessed the quiet dignity of her mother, just shrugged at Jack's most recent outburst.

"Susie and Jack, meet my friend, Pete. We work together."

"Not very choosy about who you're seen with, are you Pete?" said Jack in typical fashion.

"Nice to meet you, Pete," said Susie amiably.

"Where's the chief and the rest of the tribe?" Tony inquired.

"Steve took Dad fishing out at Fritz's. He wanted to relax before the craziness of the rest of the day. Rob is out somewhere fixing the thing-a-ma-jig on someone's watcha-ma-callit. We get a lot of requests like that from elderly customers," reported Susie.

"Yeah, and they usually buy only a couple of nuts and bolts, and give us a plate of cookies," retorted Jack.

"That's what makes this place so special," said Tony. "They may heap abuse on you, but they can fix most anything and are more than willing to try. I should know. They've bailed me out more than once. If Rob or Mike can't fix it, it's probably time for the junk pile."

Just then Mike appeared from the back where he had been making keys for a customer.

"Here's the guy who keeps all these characters in line," said Tony.

"Not really," said Mike modestly. "They'd been a successful operation long before I ever came aboard. I just give a little prod now and then."

"I told Pete our visit to Chagrin Falls wouldn't be complete without a stop at the hardware store."

"We appreciate your stopping by to say 'hello'," said Susie.

"And please come back when you're going to buy something," added Jack. "I'll tell Dad and Steve you graced us with your presence."

Tony added, "Mike, tell Patty I said 'hi'. I'll stop by for a cold one next time I'm in town."

"Anytime, Tony. You know you're always welcome."

With that, they were out the door. There was more than just a touch of regret as they left the Village behind, heading up Grove Hill. Both men were unusually quiet on the return trip, but their heads were bursting with unanswered questions and memories of the aborted Blossom Time weekend.

Finally it was Pete who broke the silence. "I couldn't help but notice. The people we met that seemed closest to you were considerably older. Do you have any buddies your age?" Realizing that he was asking questions that were actually none of his business, he quickly added, "They were all really cool folks. I don't see anything wrong with it. In fact, I'd much prefer them over most of the losers I used to hang around with."

"I realize it may be a little abnormal," Tony said in an almost apologetic tone. "I never really developed any close friendships with kids my age. I guess I was too busy worrying about the future to enjoy the present."

Pete noted a trace of regret as Tony continued.

"I wasn't an introvert or anything like that. I think most of my classmates liked me and I liked them, but we always seemed to have different priorities. Mine were more adult-oriented so I naturally gravitated toward older folks. Did I make a mistake? Probably. Do I regret missing out on being a typical teenager and would I do it differently if given a second chance? I can honestly say that I would do it exactly the same way again."

"Are you really sure about that?" asked Pete, sounding a little skeptical. "I admire practically everything about you, Tony, but there are some chinks in that armor."

They both grinned.

"I realize that. There must be if I hang around with a klutz like you!" Tony grinned as he replied.

Now they were both laughing.

"That's right. I'll make a human being out of you yet," Peter quipped.

Turning serious, Tony said sheepishly, "I know this sounds weird, but I value our friendship more than any I ever made in school."

"That's because I'm the coolest dude you ever met," joked Pete.

They sat in silence for a few miles; then it was Tony's turn to probe a bit.

"Pete, I wish you'd tell me what was troubling you so much last night. You were terrified. I get the feeling that's why we're heading back a day early."

Pete's face turned ashen, and his voice lost its usual buoyancy.

"Not now, Tony," he warned. "It's not that I don't trust you. In fact, you're the only one at that damned place I do trust." He was speaking haltingly, trying very hard to choose the proper words. "There are some things going on that I need more time to investigate before involving anyone else. I may need your help sooner than you think. Then you may be sorry you volunteered."

Tony was puzzled, but he declined to push the issue further. Maybe it was because he was afraid of what Pete would say. In any event, they were almost back.

As they rounded a bend in the road, a large but tasteful sign seemed to tower over them as they pulled onto the property.

"Welcome to Good Shepherd Funeral Home."

That evening before turning in, Tony stood looking out the window into the parking lot. He thought he saw something moving in the shadows on the opposite side of the lot. Straining his eyes, it was gone as quickly as it had appeared. He shrugged and dismissed it as his imagination. But there it was again, moving in the direction of the crematorium.

He quickly turned off the lights so he could watch without being detected. It looked like Pete, but in the darkness he couldn't be sure. There - he saw it again. The shadowy figure was definitely heading in the direction of the crematorium. He watched for another five minutes but saw nothing else. He went to bed, convinced that it had not been his imagination.

The next day Tony did not see Pete until late in the afternoon. As they passed in the hall of the main building, Tony noticed the same strange look on Pete's face he had seen the previous day.

"Hey, pal," said Tony, "let's go out tonight. Do you know a nice place in the area?"

"Gee, I'd like to, but I can't tonight," responded Pete.

Disappointed at not being able to question him about the previous night, Tony asked, "What's the matter? Are you and your girlfriend going to kiss and make up? See if she's got a friend."

"As a matter of fact, we are," responded Pete with a weak smile. "Her name's Terri, but she just took a job as a hostess with an upscale Italian restaurant in Toledo. With my crazy hours and her moving to Toledo, we'll see even less of each other than we do now, if that's possible. I guess she wants to put our relationship on hold for awhile. Maybe this absence will allow us to take a step back and see if it's important enough to both of us. Let's shoot for Friday night to let off some steam. By then I might need a shoulder to cry on," said Pete, trying to force some humor into his otherwise low spirits.

"Sounds like you two have done some serious negotiating. I hope everything works out for the best. Maybe one of these days I'll meet someone who makes me crazy like that."

"Be careful what you wish for," cautioned Pete. "At this point I'm not sure it's worth the hassle. She definitely has me crazy, but I was off to a head start before we ever met. She has just helped speed up the process. By the time Friday rolls around, my transformation should be complete." He followed with a forced laugh as he turned and headed down the hall.

Tony's eyes followed him until he disappeared around the corner. "What a character,' he thought. He may have tried to put up a good front, but it was obvious to Tony his friend was carrying a load of troubles.

The next three days were particularly busy. Then, as was typical in the funeral business, there occurred one of those inexplicable periods of inactivity. Working hours were obviously predicated by conditions over which there was no control. The only thing predictable was the unpredictability of it all.

Pete and Tony were having lunch when Pete exclaimed, "We need some R & R. Why don't we go out tonight instead of Friday? Who knows what Friday will bring!"

"Sounds good to me," agreed Tony. "We'd better take advantage of all this idle time. After those last three days, I need to get my batteries charged."

"Right on, brother," chirped Pete in a much brighter mood. "We get off duty at five, and with no calling hours scheduled, we should be able to be out of here by six. I'll sign out one of the vehicles, and we'll be on our merry way."

"See you then," said Tony excitedly as he headed over to clean the prep room. He could feel a subtle change in his personality, and he liked the feeling. Pete had been like a breath of fresh air. Tony realized that if he were going to stay in this business, he needed an attitude adjustment. His mental health was dependent upon his ability to "lighten up" during those times he wasn't wearing the undertaker's countenance. "Maybe between Don and Pete, if I'm smart enough to absorb anything, I might make a decent undertaker yet," he said to himself.

At six sharp Pete was pounding on the door and Tony came rushing out. The two bounded down the steps of his apartment like a couple of eager schoolboys.

"What took you so long?" kidded Pete. "I'm so anxious to get out of this place I almost left without you."

"If you'd have done that I'd have had Bonitto put out an APB and brought you back kicking and screaming."

"Glad to see you're loosening up just a touch," responded Pete. "There might be hope for you yet."

They both laughed and headed out to the gate. Pete rolled down the window as Stan, the guard at the gate, picked up his clipboard.

"I don't know where we're going, and I seriously doubt if we're ever coming back," he teased.

"Got it," said Stan in mock seriousness. "You two losers will be back before midnight as horny as when you left."

"I guess you've got us pretty well figured out," laughed Pete. "We're going to Nighttown for a tough steak and even tougher women."

"Now I know you'll be back before midnight if you're smart," yelled Stan as they pulled out onto the Parkway.

It was about a ten-minute drive to Nighttown. Both men took the time to unwind so very few words were spoken. It was as if they had just been paroled.

⇒➤●◄⇐

Nighttown was a favorite nightspot for Clevelanders of all ages. The decor was well worn and homey, but clean - like walking into an old friend's dimly lit living room but considerably louder. The food was good, drinks were moderately priced and the employees were well-seasoned veterans. There were two bars - almost mirror images of each other - separated by a wall. On Wednesday, Friday and Saturday, some of the better local musicians performed for a variety of musical tastes. These were many of the reasons why Nighttown was so popular. As one local patron summed it up, "You just feel comfortable here."

They entered and immediately headed for the bar.

"I really like it here," announced Pete loudly. "It's a great place to just kick back and relax."

"Any place would look good after the last three days we've put in," agreed Tony. There was a Dixieland jazz band playing loudly, and everyone was getting into the spirited mood created by these fine musicians. The next few hours literally flew by as Tony relaxed more than he had for quite awhile. He and Pete talked of many things, but Terri's name never surfaced once in their discussion. Tony felt it wasn't his place to bring it up. Just as he was about to mention what he thought he had seen the night before, Pete spoke.

"I hope we can get out again Friday," he said, suddenly becoming serious. "There are some things I'd like to talk to you about. We haven't known each other long, but I feel like we've been friends for ages. Maybe we were brothers in another life."

"I feel the same way, Pete. But why can't we talk about it now?" questioned Tony.

"This isn't the time or the place. It'll take quite awhile to tell you, and we really need to be alone. I'll tell you this much - I'm scared as hell, and I'm not ashamed to admit it. But I need to go somewhere tomorrow evening and I'd rather not discuss anything now. Friday will be soon enough if things go as I hope."

The strained look that Tony had previously noticed became more clearly one of anxiety. Tony desperately wanted to ask him what was troubling him but forced himself not to pry. If he had only known Pete better, he would have pressed for an explanation right on the spot. He only went so far as to say, "If there is anything you ever want to talk about, I'm good at listening."

"Thanks, I really appreciate that," said Pete. "This is something I need to do on my own. I don't want to get you involved at this point." His usual high-spirited attitude was gone. He seemed to be preoccupied with something. Tony realized that further discussion was fruitless.

"Let's head for the barn, Pete," he suggested. "We've both had a long day." Business could pick up as quickly as it had vanished, and both men were painfully aware of this fact.

"Good idea," said Pete with little emotion in his voice. During the ride back he was uncommunicative. His thoughts were elsewhere, and Tony respected his retreat into himself. It was clear to him that something was troubling Pete far more than a lover's spat.

———»•○•«———

Tony did not cross paths with Pete at all the next day. Tony had to drive to City Hall to get several death certificate copies. He didn't especially enjoy the job, and the line was longer than usual. "I wonder who fouled up today?" thought Tony. "Whoever it was, I'm sure they blamed someone else. Oh well - you can't fight City Hall!"

After a frustrating hour at the counter, Tony headed back to the funeral home. As he drove he couldn't get his mind off Pete's change in behavior. Thinking back over the days since they met, Pete's moods had certainly been erratic. "Maybe it's just his personality. After all, I really don't know him that well, and he doesn't know me well enough to confide in me yet. It really does take awhile to develop trust and confidence in someone," Tony thought.

"Whatever!" he muttered in resignation as he turned into the long drive.

It was almost dark when he stopped at the gate. Stan wasn't at the Gate House.

"Where's Stan?" Tony asked.

"His wife is sick. He went home early," replied the stranger, never looking up as he checked Tony in.

"I didn't know he was married."

"Look friend," said the guard, somewhat irritated. "That's what they said when they called me in. I just do what I'm told and don't ask questions. If you have a problem with this, check it out at the main office." He was now staring at him with the coldest gray eyes Tony had ever seen. His piercing stare was quite menacing, and Tony recoiled slightly.

He mumbled, "No big deal," and drove off. "Sure hope this guy is not a permanent replacement. He doesn't exactly give the impression of a friendly greeter at the gate - more like a troll!" He smiled at his rare attempt at humor.

He took the death certificates to the office but couldn't resist carrying his investigation a bit farther. As he placed the certificates on the desk, Tony asked the attendant, "What happened? Why did Stan get the night off?"

"Search me," he said. "Mr. Bonitto gave him the night off. He personally handles security. Maybe he wanted to break in a new guy."

"Just curious," said Tony. "Seems like a strange time to make a change."

"It's none of my business, and I don't ask. You'd do well to follow the same policy," cautioned the attendant with a slightly ominous tone to his voice.

"Anything left for supper?" asked Tony, changing the subject.

"I think so, but you'd better hurry," he said as he took the "certifieds" to the inner office.

The cafeteria was empty, but there was enough food left to make a meal. He really wasn't very hungry. There were too many things on his mind. Where had Pete gone? Who was the new guard? Why did he take over in the middle of a shift? Who was the person he'd seen the other night? What was he doing lurking in the shadows at such a late hour?

Mulling all these questions had distracted Tony to the extent that he hadn't even touched his food. He snapped back to the present, downed his glass of milk, took some cookies and trudged up to his apartment. His mind was whirling, but he had to get some sleep.

⟫•●•⟪

It was 3 a.m. when the black station wagon passed through the gates of Good Shepherd. The headlights were off as it silently glided into the parking lot. The car proceeded to the rear of the lot and backed up to the entrance of the crematorium. Two men got out, walked to the rear of the wagon, opened the tailgate, slid the gurney quickly out and entered the building. A few minutes later they reappeared, got in the car and drove off into the night.

A short time later the door opened. A tall figure emerged and slowly walked the length of the parking lot. The lights illuminated the face of Carlo Bonitto as he paused to extinguish a cigarette. No sooner had he entered the building than something moved in the darkness opposite Tony's apartment. It moved silently, darting in and out of shadows, heading toward the crematorium.

———⊸◦⊷———

Tony woke up, took a shower and headed for breakfast. Pete was sitting at one of the tables and Tony joined him.

"Everything go all right last night?" asked Tony, not really expecting an explanation.

"Better than expected," mumbled Pete in a hushed tone. "Let's hope we can get out tonight; we need to talk." He spoke without even looking at Tony. It was as though he didn't want to draw attention to their conversation.

"I know I can trust you, Tony," he continued, still without looking up. "I have something very important to ask you. I don't think we should leave together. I'll meet you at Nighttown tonight at seven-thirty."

"Can I ask you one question, Pete? Just give me a yes or no. Were you sneaking down to the crematorium a few nights ago?"

"Yes, and last night too!" said Pete as he got up and left the table without another word.

Tony remained at the table too stunned to move. He had half expected this response, but the truth of it left him in shock. Problems with Pete's love life were insignificant compared to this latest development.

—————

The rest of the day was uneventful, but Tony could not erase that last exchange with Pete. Something was very wrong, and he was anxious to find out what it was. Though he hadn't a clue why, he was developing a very uneasy feeling over what the evening might reveal.

Tony arrived at the restaurant early. He hadn't seen Pete all day and was nervously waiting to hear what he had to tell him. By eight-thirty he started to worry. After another half-hour had passed, he decided to go to Pete's apartment. If Pete were coming, he surely would have been here by now. He tried to shrug off his concerns, assuming Pete must have been called to perform some task at work. That was not out of the ordinary. He reasoned nothing more could be accomplished by waiting any longer so he left Nighttown, got in his car and headed back.

As he drove he began imagining all sorts of things, none of which gave him an overwhelming feeling of confidence regarding Pete's absence. He entered the gates. There was Stan as usual.

"Missed your smiling face last night, Stan," said Tony, trying to appear casual.

"Happens every once in a while. Mr. Bonitto gives me the night off. Nice guy!" said Stan matter-of-factly.

"It's great to get an unexpected break like that," offered Tony. "I'll bet your wife appreciated it."

Never had that pleasure," responded Stan. "Been a lone wolf all these years. It's not fair to womankind to tie myself to just one."

"Right," mocked Tony. "By the way, Stan, what time did Pete check out?"

"Never saw hide nor hair of him this evening."

"This is getting more and more weird by the minute," thought Tony. He had an uneasy feeling as he drove into the garage under his apartment.

He hurried over to Pete's even though the apartment was dark. He pounded on the door and tried the knob. It wasn't locked so he cautiously entered. The hair on the back of his neck began to bristle as he made his way around the dimly lit apartment. He called out, but there was only silence. Now he was really worried. He decided to leave a note on the table for Pete and go back to his own apartment.

Tony propped himself up in a chair so he could see out the window. From there he could watch Pete's apartment and hopefully wait for his arrival. He settled in for a nervous vigil. His stomach was churning with dread. He sensed something far more serious than a midnight run for a body but tried to dismiss his fears.

"It'll all be explained in the morning," he reasoned.

<hr />

He twitched and his eyes snapped open. It was daylight. There had been no word from Pete. Tony's note had asked him to come over as soon as he arrived home. He rushed over to Pete's apartment and tried the door. It was locked.

"It's a good sign," he thought. "He probably got home late and didn't want to disturb me." He returned to his own apartment, quickly showered, dressed and went to breakfast, expecting to find Pete there. He was only slightly alarmed not to find him.

"Must have slept in or is already out on an assignment," Tony soothed himself. "I'm sure to bump into him sometime today." The thought didn't harbor a great deal of conviction.

The day passed with no contact from Pete, and the sick feeling he'd been fighting off intensified. By evening, when no lights appeared in Pete's apartment, he began to really worry.

"There's probably a very logical explanation," he

decided. He tried to be patient, occupying his mind by writing a long overdue letter home. He nervously paced the apartment for another half-hour, then tried unsuccessfully to watch TV. The waiting was driving him crazy. His nerves couldn't take much more of this. Something had to be terribly wrong.

Finally, when he could take the waiting no longer, he rushed over to Josh's apartment and knocked. When Josh opened the door, Tony barged in before being invited. Somewhat taken back by the intrusion, Josh quickly regained his composure.

"What's the problem, Tony?" he asked, seeing the worried look on his face.

"I hope it's nothing, but I'm concerned because I haven't seen Pete since Thursday afternoon."

"Come to think of it, I haven't either," agreed Josh. "I just assumed he was working where I wasn't. I often go for a day without seeing him."

"Could you get a key so we can check his room?" pleaded Tony, practically pushing Josh out the door.

"Wait! My master key is on the dresser," said Josh, pulling out of Tony's grasp. He reappeared, and the two men hurried over to Pete's apartment. When they entered, Tony immediately noticed that the note he had left was still in its original place. He quickly slid his hand over it. He was sure Josh had not seen him. Hopefully no one else had seen the note. A thorough search showed that Pete had not been there all day. Tony's fears were confirmed. He began to believe he'd never see his friend again.

"Let me check with the main office to see if he is out on a call. I'll get back to you as soon as I hear anything," assured Josh.

Tony went to his apartment and waited for what seemed an eternity. A knock on the door caused his heart to leap in his chest. He sprang to his feet and rushed to the door to confront Josh.

"He's vanished," said Josh. "No one knows a thing. It seems you were the last one seen talking to him."

Tony's jaw dropped. He couldn't believe what he was hearing. Though he was used to dealing with death, it was impersonal. He was not prepared for what Josh had just said.

"Did he say anything that might help us find him?"

"Not a thing," lied Tony. "I was hoping you had better news than this."

"Sorry," said Josh, "but we'll continue searching."

"Was there anyone in his family you could call?" asked Tony.

"His records indicate he had no family; we're at a dead end there. We don't know anyone we can contact," said Josh. "We'll call the authorities immediately." He started out the door, then casually turned to Tony.

"Oh yes, I almost forgot - did he ever mention a girl? I think her name was Toni or Terri."

"Sorry, Josh, I never heard him say anything about a girl." He didn't feel comfortable providing Josh with answers, especially after his last exchange with Pete.

"Well, thanks, it was probably nothing," he said as he turned and left.

"Very convenient," thought Tony. "Whatever happened will not result in his family pushing for a thorough investigation. Josh seemed concerned. But my guess is he knows more than he's letting on. Someone called Toni or Terri - not a very convincing act."

He tried to dismiss his suspicions with a shrug, but his overactive imagination was onto something although he hadn't a clue what. He knew Pete had discovered something dangerous enough to admittedly frighten him. Did he fear for his life? Had he discovered something that resulted in his disappearance? Was there a connection between his strange behavior and activities at Good Shepherd? There were so many questions, and no one to help him find answers. Pete had said that he, Tony, was the only person he could trust. Having been there almost a year, Pete had to know what he was talking about.

If he tried to find out what had been scaring Pete, there was the possibility he would experience the same fate as his friend. The thought of it made him sick to his stomach. He was not a coward, but he really had nowhere to turn. He was frustrated, confused and more than a little frightened.

12

A full week passed. The lack of any news only accelerated Tony's anxieties. The police and Bonitto had questioned the staff. Various theories were proposed, but each ended with the same result - nothing. Tony desperately wanted to know what the authorities had discovered, but he masked his curiosity. He was about to explode, and he was afraid everyone noticed it, especially Bonitto.

"How could Pete just flat out disappear?" Tony kept asking himself. "Too many things just don't add up, especially when we had arranged to meet that evening. I wish I knew what he wanted to tell me. There has to be some connection. Who else knew about our meeting?" He couldn't erase the look on Pete's face. There was no mistaking the fear in his eyes.

Tony tried to tie together all the unrelated incidents from the previous weeks. Everything seemed to point to some connection between what Pete had discovered about activities at Good Shepherd and his mysterious disappearance. What Pete had discovered and what had happened to him were consuming Tony's thoughts night and day. It appeared that the authorities had no more leads to pursue, at least for the time being. All indications seemed to confirm that Good Shepherd had concluded its investigation as well.

He was now sure that any more answers would require his taking matters into his own hands. Where could he start? The only possibility Tony could come up with was there might be some clue left in Pete's apartment. The door had been left unlocked initially so it was possible that Pete had returned. The fact that it was found locked when he checked had to have some significance.

He had to get into that apartment without drawing any suspicion.

Tony decided he'd go to Josh with some excuse and hope he was believable enough. It appeared to be his only option so it was worth a try. Later that day Tony found Josh.

"I need to ask you a favor," he began. "I lent Pete some of my CD's, and I was wondering if you would let me have the key so I could get them back."

"No problem," said Josh, "we can go over right now."

Tony hoped his disappointment didn't show. "Sounds good. I could go. It'll only take a minute," he said. Maybe Josh would decide it wasn't worth his time to accompany him. Unfortunately, it didn't work. Together they went to the apartment. Tony went to the CD rack, pretending to sort through it. He selected two. He and Josh started to leave, but Tony stopped abruptly in the doorway.

"I just remembered there was one more," he lied. "It'll only take a second. I'll lock the door on my way out." He rushed back in before Josh could respond, grabbed the first CD he saw and quickly returned to the door. Turning his back to Josh, he pretended to lock the door, but didn't push in the button on the inside handle. He pulled the door shut and faked checking it to make sure it was locked. He thanked Josh and headed for his apartment.

"This is going to make things a little more difficult," he thought.

Tony could never remember being this nervous at anytime in his entire life. He could not keep his hands from shaking, but he knew this was something he had to do. He waited impatiently until it was dark enough to make his move. The parking lot was fairly well illuminated, but the space between the security lights created several shadow zones throughout the perimeter. His plan was to circle around the back of the buildings, go to the end of the lot and come up the outer side. The only time he would be vulnerable was when he was in front of Pete's building and when he had to climb the stairs to the apartment. Fortunately there was no direct light, but anyone looking in that direction was sure to see him. He had to chance it. It would take less than five seconds to climb the stairs and enter the room.

The door was still unlocked; at least he'd fooled Josh. All the curtains and shades were drawn so there would be no indication of activity inside. He withdrew a small flashlight and began scanning the main room. He stopped abruptly and went over to the door. "Better lock it just in case," he whispered aloud. He had no idea what he was looking for or where to begin.

After a thorough search, he discovered nothing that could remotely be considered a clue. He was feeling very inadequate at this detective business. His courses in criminology certainly weren't helping him much with the investigation.

He froze as he heard a sound just as he was about to leave. He heard voices outside. It sounded like people were coming up the stairs. There could only be one place they were heading - Pete's apartment. As he heard the key slide into the lock, he dropped to his stomach and slid under the bed just as the door opened.

Two men entered the room, but Tony didn't recognize the voices.

"I'll take care of the phone and you pull the bug from the ceiling fixture," said a man with a high-pitched voice.

"Right," said the other. "I wonder why he waited so long to get this stuff out of here?"

"I don't know and I don't ask," replied the first man. "Just get it done and let's get out of here. I guess they're going to clean and paint tomorrow cause someone else will be moving in soon. I hope he's not too smart for his own good like this last guy. Make sure you lock it; we don't want that snoop from the other building coming in again."

It seemed like forever for them to complete the job although it was actually only a few minutes, and they were out the door. As it closed, Tony let out a gasp so loud he was afraid they had heard him. He remained under the bed as he tried to calm his racing heart and regain his composure. A terrifying thought pierced him like a knife. "What if I'm next," he thought as he shuddered at the prospect.

Lying there, he tried to think of any possible thing he might have overlooked. He remembered the note pad he had used to leave the message for Pete. It was a long shot, but sometimes impressions from previous notes are left on the paper. He slid out, grabbed the notepad and peeked out through an opening in the drapes. The parking lot appeared to be deserted. Tony opened the door and slipped down the stairs as quickly as possible. He retraced his steps back to his apartment. He took the stairs two at a time and burst into his room undetected.

He collapsed on the bed and lay there. He could not stop shaking. He went over his recent escapade in his mind and began to calm down. Suddenly he sat up. In his panic he had forgotten to lock the door! He jumped up from the bed. Looking out the window, he froze in his tracks. There, across the lot, was a black station wagon parked right below Pete's apartment.

Tony remained standing in the darkened room. He strained his eyes, searching for any signs of activity. Presently the door opened and three men emerged from the apartment. They moved quickly, making it impossible to identify them. They descended the stairs and approached the car. As they opened the door, the interior lights illuminated them briefly. Tony could not believe his eyes. The man in the middle quickly looked up at him. The face appeared bloodied and puffy, but there was no mistake - it was Pete! Tony stood in stunned silence as the car left the lot.

"They must have been desperate to chance returning at this hour," he reasoned. Snapping back to his senses, still not believing what he had seen, he rushed out of the room, grabbed the first car he saw and sped toward the main gate.

As he approached the Gate House, an alarming sight met him. It was the stranger who had manned the gate last week. This could not be a coincidence. Tony forced himself to relax as he pulled up to the window.

"Tony Amico, just going to McDonald's. Be back in half an hour," he said trying to act as nonchalant as possible. The stranger nodded and wrote something as he acknowledged his presence.

By the time Tony had left the grounds, the station wagon was no longer in sight. He hadn't the slightest idea in which direction they might have gone.

"This is stupid," he said to himself. "Those guys aren't amateurs; they've obviously covered their tracks well. I might as well head back. I can't accomplish anything driving around in circles." Then he thought of something. Slamming on the brakes he made a U-turn and sped off in the opposite direction.

There was a possibility that they had taken Pete to the Scarletto compound. It was a stretch, but it was the only option. Tony remembered the location from when Pete had pointed it out one day. He turned onto Murray Hill, heading toward the fortress just off Mayfield Road. He wasn't sure what he would do when he got there. As far as entering the grounds for the purpose of snooping around, that had to be totally out of the question. "Why am I even doing this?" he wondered.

He approached a formidable structure surrounded by a solid brick wall that must have been 8 feet high and several feet thick. "What is this, the Berlin wall?" he wondered. "I'd need a full platoon of Green Berets and a Sherman tank to crash this place."

He slowed down as he approached the tall stone pillars anchoring an impressive wrought iron gate. Surveillance devices were perched on the top of each pillar. Their electronic eyes pivoted slowly. There was no evidence of anyone in the immediate area. Tony slowed down, straining his eyes, searching through the gate into the dimly lit grounds. Nothing.

He turned the corner and headed up a darkened side street. "This place is awesome," he observed. "It must be every bit as big as Good Shepherd."

———➤•◦•◄———

Inside the Scarletto mansion an elderly man had been watching a television monitor. Slowly turning away, he called out, "Get Carlo on the phone right away."

———➤•◦•◄———

Turning onto a narrow, rubble-strewn alley, Tony made his way along the back of the estate. The only light other than his headlights was a sporadic flash that must have come from security lights at the rear of the house. The light danced faintly in thin shafts as a breeze continuously stirred the leaves in the dense overgrowth. Though the front was immaculately landscaped, the rear appeared untouched. The street was obviously neglected. By its appearance, the city hadn't maintained it for years. Branches and leaves struggled to escape through the tall, rusted chain-link fence. On the opposite side was a stone retaining wall that formed the distant border of Lake View Cemetery. Tony had been there a few times but had never seen this section nor noticed the estate on its border. Both sides of the alley were so overgrown that a car could barely fit through. Branches occasionally extended out into the alley, brushing against the sides of his car.

As Tony swerved to avoid one of the larger branches, the headlights danced across a small break in the pattern along the fence. He stopped the car, and using his flashlight, cautiously inspected this area more closely. The vegetation had been cut recently, just enough to expose a small gate. Whoever had done the work had neglected to snap the rusted padlock and had left it dangling on an equally rusty chain. The security of the fortress had been left vulnerable due to someone's negligence.

The only question was whether Tony had the guts (or stupidity) to take advantage of this breach. He had to find out if Pete were a captive of the Scarlettos.

Summoning up all his courage, he forced the creaky gate open wide enough to slip past. Sharp twig ends scratched and clawed as if to say, "Stay out if you know what's good for you."

Failing to heed the warning, he stumbled in as tentacle-like vines wrapped around his ankles almost tripping him. Even though it was an unseasonably cool evening, Tony could feel nervous perspiration soaking his thin cotton shirt. In the faint light he could make out a large garage area about one hundred yards away. It covered the entire rear of the house. As he struggled toward the light, he had the sensation that he was not alone. His premonition became reality as he came to a halt. Every hair on his body bristled as he came face to face with the largest dog he had ever seen. A guttural growl emerged through curled lips that exposed intimidating fangs. Obviously this was not Buster, the family pet.

Neither moved for what seemed like agonizing minutes. Finally Tony made a slow, half step backward. This attempt was met with a growl of increased ferocity though the dog did not move. Tony stopped abruptly, tried to calm his racing heart and put his brain into gear. If he turned and ran, the "Hound from hell" could easily catch him and most likely knock him down with the force of its one-hundred eighty plus pounds. Once on the ground he would be chopped liver.

It was at least twenty yards through tangled underbrush to the gate. Squeezing through the narrow opening would take precious moments and leave him vulnerable. Another factor enhanced his already precarious situation. How long would it be before his presence was detected by someone in the house? He had to act and act fast. In an obvious no-win situation, which poison did he want?

How could he possibly outsmart or outmaneuver the four-legged menace? The dog was trained to do exactly what he was doing and no doubt was quite good at it. Tony's only weapon was a 6-inch flashlight which was about like going against a charging rhino with a BB-gun.

Out of the corner of his eye he spied a rather formidable-looking section of a broken limb. It was no more than a foot away, but he couldn't tell its condition. With his luck, it was so rotten that it would fall apart when he tried to pick it up. He had three rather dubious choices: (1) Run like hell and pray he could reach the fence and get through it before Buster reacted. Scratch 1! (2) Go on the attack and bludgeon man's best friend senseless with a six-inch flashlight. Scratch 2! (3) Distract his canine antagonist long enough to grab the log. Assuming it was somewhat durable, he'd bust him alongside the head and then run like hell. Option 3 didn't overwhelm him with confidence, but it was the best of the three.

Trying to calm a quivering hand, he slowly raised the flashlight and directed it at the dog. Now or never! He turned on the beam and aimed it directly in the animal's eyes. Momentarily confused by the light, Brutus failed to react as Tony quickly grabbed the small log. To his relief it felt sturdy in his grasp - and none too soon. The dog quickly regained its sense and moved aggressively to attack. With a menacing growl that exposed lethal fangs, he sprang directly at Tony's throat. Anticipating this move, Tony quickly stepped back, dropped the flashlight and gripped the branch with both hands. The dog's leap fell short as Tony took a cut that would've done Babe Ruth proud. His adrenaline-laced swing caught the dog with its full force across the left side of its face and head. With a loud whimper, it fell to the ground, stunned by the impact.

Tony turned and began running the longest twenty yards of his life. Under ideal conditions it would be a photo finish. Now he had to contend with the thick undergrowth trying to trip him up every agonizing step of the way. Though his ears were pounding, he thought he heard the dog crashing behind him. He didn't dare look back. Fractions of seconds were crucial. He raced toward the gate just a few yards away. Luckily he was running straight for the opening so he wouldn't have to slow down. Like a sprinter straining for the finish line, he hurled his body through the air, scraping both arms against the sharp edges of the small opening.

Tony lay in a heap, the sides of his shirt torn to shreds. He rolled over on his back. Instinctively he raised both feet and savagely kicked at the gate. It slammed shut just as the dog's head was entering and hit him directly on the nose. A loud yelp told Tony he had time to reach the safety of the car. He opened the door and dove inside. There was no time to relax as the dog's next leap caught the door and miraculously slammed it shut. Tony looked in terror as the crazed beast clawed and snapped at the glass barrier. He feverishly turned the key to the sweet sound of the motor turning over. In his panic he had neglected to turn on the headlights. A brief flash of light told him he was headed directly for the stone retaining wall. Veering quickly to the right, he drove off, leaving the dog standing in the darkness.

He was a mess, both emotionally and physically. There was no way he could return to the funeral home in this state. He would also have to come up with a good story to explain the condition of the car. First things first. He had to get himself together and look somewhat presentable.

He drove to the shelter house in the Metropark. The rest rooms were open all night so he could clean himself up to some degree. He removed his torn shirt and deposited it in the trash receptacle. Fortunately his T-shirt was completely in tact. After he got through the gate, he could most likely get into his apartment unnoticed. The car would be another matter. Hopefully it was not as bad as he feared.

Returning to the funeral home, he nervously nodded to the stranger as he passed through the gate. Not only was he dealing with the disappearance of Pete, but he now had to be concerned about his own safety. Any illusion he had about not drawing unnecessary attention was long gone. He would have to be keenly aware of any change in attitude toward him, even the slightest indication that he was under suspicion.

"What was so important that they would have risked bringing Pete back to the apartment?" queried Tony. "They must have gotten some information out of him judging from the looks of his face." At least Pete was alive for now - but for how long?

As he turned into his garage the headlights illuminated someone standing directly in his path - the last person in the world he wanted to see - Carlo Bonitto.

"I was looking for you earlier," said a stony-faced Carlo. "Joseph told me you had left the grounds. I must have just missed you."

"Yeah, I had a Big Mac attack," said Tony, trying to appear casual while not looking directly at him. "How can I help you?"

"We had a call a short time ago. We need you to drive to Stevens Funeral Home in Warren for a pickup," said Carlo. "They said they'd wait up for us so you have to leave immediately. Are you sure you can make the trip? You seem unusually tired."

He hoped Carlo had not detected anything and was just probing.

"No problem - I'm on my way," he said, trying his best to appear casual. If Carlo noticed anything unusual about the car, he didn't reveal it. "Maybe it's not so bad looking after all. This guy usually doesn't miss a thing," Tony thought.

"Here are the directions and paperwork you'll need; have a safe trip," said Carlo, never changing his expression. As he handed the package through the car's window, Tony drove slowly over to the garage, hoping to give Bonitto time to retreat to the main building.

The hearse was gassed up and ready so Tony left without even entering his apartment. He gave a great sigh of relief and stepped on the gas. As soon as he reached a BP gas station on Cedar Road, he stopped at the pay phone. It was only 10:30 so there was plenty of time. He punched in the number.

The phone rang four times before someone at the other end picked up the receiver. To his relief a male voice answered.

"Uncle Gino, this is Tony," he said excitedly. "I'm on my way to Warren. Can you meet me at the Raintree in two hours?"

"What's the problem, Tony?" asked Gino.

"I have to talk to you. I can't explain now, but it's important," said Tony. "You know I wouldn't ask you to do this if it wasn't. I have to pick up a body so I should be there by 12:30. I realize you'll be missing your beauty sleep, but I have to see you."

⊱•◦•⊰

"You can count on me," said Gino. "You know it's going to cost you a cup of coffee or two."

"Gladly," said Tony. "And one other thing - please don't tell Mama we talked. Thanks a million." He hung up, jumped in the hearse and sped off heading for Warren.

There were no delays on the way and everything went smoothly at Stevens. Tony was able to arrive at Raintree on time. As he entered, Uncle Gino rushed up and gave him a big hug. His face showed obvious concern, making him look older than his fifty-plus years.

"You sounded so anxious on the phone. I've been here for forty-five minutes and already downed two cups of coffee," said Gino. "You want to give your Uncle Gino a heart attack? Business can't be so bad that you have to go out and recruit customers."

"Why would I want to give my favorite uncle a heart attack?" teased Tony, trying to hide his anxiety.

"You mean your only uncle," retorted Gino. "Now tell me, what's so important that I had to drive here in the middle of the night?" Turning semi-serious he said, "You know I'd do anything for my favorite and only nephew."

"You may be sorry you said that, Uncle Gino. I have to ask you some things I know you won't want to tell me." The seriousness in his tone told Gino that small-talk time was over.

"I need you to betray a confidence that was entrusted to you a long time ago," said Tony. "I wouldn't ask you if it was not possibly a matter of life and death. Uncle Gino, I need to know what happened to my father."

Gino's face went blank. He lowered his eyes and began shaking his head back and forth. "I told your mama it was a mistake to let you go to 'that place', but she wanted you to have the chance your papa never got. I'll burn in hell for what I am about to tell you and your mama will throw extra coal in."

"Like I said, Uncle Gino..."

"Yes, I know," interrupted Gino, "and if it weren't a matter of life or death, I would take it to my grave. Prepare yourself for something that is going to knock you on your ass. Your real last name is Scarletto." Tony could not believe what he had just heard. He fought the urge to interrupt as Gino continued. "Your mama changed her name after moving to Chagrin. Your papa joined Good Shepherd Funeral Home just after the war. He was only sixteen when he came from Sicily to work for them. Though he was a distant relative, he proved himself to be very dependable and quickly got their attention.

"As the years passed he became a trusted member of the Family's inner circle. He learned more and more about the true sources of their wealth as they involved him in the secret Family operations. Your mama was a distant cousin who was brought over several years later to work as a domestic. They met, fell in love and were married all within a year. You were born the following year." Tony blinked in disbelief.

Gino continued. "It seems a member of the Family was suspected of going public. Before they could do anything to quiet him, he disappeared. They called your papa in after it was discovered where they were hiding him. To show his gratitude and loyalty to the Scarletto Family, he was to quiet the informer permanently. In return, if anything happened, they promised to provide your mama with a generous income for life. Obviously this was a no-win situation for your papa, but he was a loyal soldier. Even if his attempt were successful, it would almost certainly result in his death or, at the very least, years behind bars.

"An informant who worked in a local hospital told the Scarlettos the police had him in the Cleveland Clinic. They plotted the assassination. Thanks to your papa the plan was carried out, and the potential threat to the Family was eliminated.

"Though your papa was able to carry out his assignment successfully, he was captured in the process. Attempts to get him to talk were unsuccessful. In fact, he refused to speak a single word during the trial. He went to prison without ever opening his mouth. Three years later your mama received a letter saying he had been murdered in the prison's laundry room. They never found out who did it, though we had our suspicions.

"By that time your mama had moved to Chagrin Falls and was living with us. My wife, your Aunt Ellie, died when Albert was born. Your mama took over as the woman of our household and was like a mother to your cousins. Every check she received from the Family was put in a savings account in your name. She made me swear on my wife's grave never to tell you the true source of the money. I still can't understand why she didn't try to stop you from going to work for them. I know it really upset her. You knew this too."

"Maybe she felt they owed us," said Tony disbelievingly as he slumped back in his chair. "I'm sure that's why they offered me a job. Now it makes sense; I never could understand why they picked me out in the first place."

"I want you to understand that your father was an honorable man. His first duty and responsibility was to your mother and you. His second was to the Family. He had a strong sense of loyalty to both of you and to the Family. As you very well know, family and loyalty are everything to an Italian. Your father did what he needed to do to be true to himself." Uncle Gino drew a deep breath.

"Thank you, Uncle Gino. I needed to know that. It helps. It's a lot to take in. And don't worry, Mama will never know of our conversation. Thanks so much for telling me everything. I had to know. I still have a lot of unanswered questions, but at least I'm beginning to make some sense out of this whole mess. I'd better get going. I'm sure they are keeping track of time. I'll need a good excuse for my late arrival."

"There's one more piece of information you need to know. This is the hardest part. Mr. Scarletto is your Godfather. Not just 'The Godfather', but yours when you were baptized. You were named for him. Through the years he would go to school events, wrestling meets - whenever you were involved in something that he could attend. He used to come to our house when you were little and play with you. He gave you your first wagon, your first tricycle and your first baseball. I was afraid you might recognize him, even if he has aged."

Tony was stunned. He was certain that the older man he'd seen at his graduation and the restaurant in Little Italy was his Godfather. Now he knew why he thought he'd known him and why the man had seemed so kindly to him. He must have some memory of him from his childhood, and the memory was good!

Gino had tears in his eyes as they rose to leave. "Be careful my only nephew," he said. His parting hug told more than any words. Tony was afraid he might never see this wonderful man again, and he sensed Uncle Gino shared his fears.

As he drove back to Good Shepherd, Tony's mind was in a whirl. Uncle Gino's revelation had created a mental tug-of-war. His own father had been a part of it. Yet he had been a loving and caring husband and father. And he had been honorable. How could he, Tony, rationalize what his father had done, yet still respect him? How could his godfather, a man who could be so cruel and heartless, also be so kind and caring? Could Tony, whose standards of conduct were above reproach, respect a person who lived outside the law? Would all those years of doing the "right thing" become meaningless if he accepted the Godfather and what he stood for? Tony knew he couldn't have it both ways. But he also knew that family and loyalty and honor were as deeply ingrained in who he was as his sense of right and wrong. Even his second choice of career, in criminology, reflected that. There was no gray area between good and evil. A lifetime of strong convictions left no room for compromise.

Tony gritted his teeth and prepared for wherever his decision would lead him.

———=❖=———

After taking care of business at the office, Tony pulled the hearse up to the prep room and wheeled the gurney in. He was relieved to learn another employee was scheduled to embalm his passenger. Gratefully he returned to his apartment, still in a trance. As soon as he entered, he had the eerie feeling that someone had been in his room during his absence. Remembering the discussion of the two men in Pete's apartment, he automatically looked at the phone. He removed the jack from the wall and took the receiver from its cradle. Unscrewing the mouthpiece, he saw a small metallic object attached to the diaphragm.

"I'm no electronic wizard, but if this isn't a phone tap I'm sadly mistaken," he thought as he returned everything to its original condition.

"They may suspect me, but they can't be sure Pete ever confided in me. In any event, I have to be on my guard. There may be too much at stake for them to take a chance on whether I know anything or not. I can only hope I know more about them than they know about me."

He took a shower and got into bed. In spite of the fact it was 3:00 a.m., he could not sleep. His mind was racing. What was he to do? Should he wait for them to make the next move? If he waited, their next move might be his last.

He finally drifted off in an uneasy sleep.

⸻⸻

The next day proved to be uneventful as Tony searched for any hint that might indicate a change in their attitude. Pushing his luck, he went out of his way to run into Bonitto.

"I hope everything was all right since that was my first solo road trip," queried Tony.

"Everything was fine, and you made good time," answered Carlo.

Tony thought he detected a faint trace of a smile. He allowed himself a slight feeling of relief for the first time in over twenty-four hours.

"You'd better get a good night's sleep. You look like you could use it," said Carlo. "Is anything bothering you?"

Bonitto's question jolted him. He couldn't afford to let his guard down, not for one second.

"The trip must have made me more nervous than I realized," he lied. "I did have trouble sleeping last night."

"Don't worry about being on call tonight, Tony," said Carlo. "Get some rest; we need to have our employees looking a bit more alert than you do right now."

"Thanks," said Tony, smiling. "I'll take you up on that; don't want to hurt the corporate image."

He walked away feeling considerably better than he did before talking to Bonitto. They may be suspicious, but somehow he sensed he was not immediately in jeopardy. Maybe they bug all the phones, and it could have been there from the beginning. That wouldn't explain why they removed the bugs from Pete's apartment. Though he felt better, he quickly resumed trying to answer questions. His success rate was no better than before, but at least he knew what had happened to his father and why Good Shepherd had chosen him to employ.

Now he needed to think about his father. He was trying hard to understand how loyalty could sometimes make a person deviate from the straight and narrow. But then where does a person draw the line? Honor above all? Honor to whom? And how could he turn in his godfather, the man who had acted with honor toward Tony's own family. Didn't Tony owe him loyalty?

More confused than ever, Tony turned his thoughts to the problem that was more pressing at the moment - Pete. Why was he abducted? What did he have on them? Was it serious enough to be life threatening? Based on what he had discovered from Uncle Gino, he was not very optimistic regarding Pete's chances of survival. He had an idea that might lessen their suspicions of him and buy him a little more time in the process.

Since he was certain they had tapped his phone, he just might be able to use it to his advantage. Quickly returning to his room, he dialed a familiar number and was relieved to hear Don's voice.

"Stroud-Lawrence Funeral Home, this is Don. How can we help you?"

"Don, it's Tony."

"Hey Judi, pick up the extension. It's our Italian Stallion," he shouted happily.

"Hi, Tony," chimed in Judi. "We thought you'd fallen into a black hole or something."

"I'm sorry. They've kept me super busy. I've hardly had time to catch my breath. I've got a short break so I wanted to call and update you on what's happening here. I really miss you guys, but the experience I'm getting is invaluable."

"Now I suppose you're going to expect a big raise when you finish your apprenticeship," joked Don. "I assume you are still planning on returning, if you know what's good for you."

"I really like it here and they treat me just fine," he lied, "but my heart and loyalties will always be in Chagrin Falls. This place is awesome, and I'm learning a part of the business I never even knew existed." Actually this was not too far from the truth; however, those were things that could not be discussed if he expected to remain among the living.

"Sounds like you'll be able to teach me a few new twists," quipped Don. "When are you going to get some time off so we can compare notes?"

"You ought to know how that goes by now, Don. Didn't you once tell me 'time off' was not in an undertaker's vocabulary?"

"I take it you've become irreplaceable already. They better not burn you out before I get a chance to," warned Don.

"Don't worry, this Italian Stallion will still have enough left for you to exploit."

"Be sure to take care of yourself," cautioned Judi. "Get your rest and eat at least one decent meal a week."

"Yes, Mother," laughed Tony. "I'll be sure to have my cookies and milk before I turn in at the usual 9:30 lights out. Well, I really do have to get back to the grind. It was great talking to you both. I'll call again soon.'

After hanging up, he felt fairly confident their seemingly innocent conversation had served its purpose.

A fine mist intensified the gloom. Swirling around the security lights, the scene only needed the lonesome wail of a foghorn to make it complete.

A black station wagon slipped quietly around the corner of the building. The headlights were out as it glided through the murk. Approaching the rear of the lot, it stopped and maneuvered into position. The driver and his passenger got out, opened the tailgate and removed the gurney. Straps surrounded a deep maroon body bag. The entire length was tightly sealed. They quickly entered the building, closing out the light. Several minutes later they reappeared and left as silently as they had come.

A short time later the door opened again. The form in the doorway cast a long shadow halfway across the parking lot. Then it was dark once more.

Carlo Bonitto walked slowly toward the main building. In his hand was a small journal.

Fortunately, Tony had concealed the notepad in his apartment. Had he left it in plain sight there was a good chance his lone piece of potential evidence would be gone for good. He sat at his desk with a bright light over his left shoulder. He strained his eyes as he slowly studied each page. It quickly became obvious that he would gain no information from them. If there were any impression on the pages, it would definitely require a more sophisticated method of detection.

He stopped abruptly when he reached the cardboard backing. He had almost missed it - there, in the upper right corner of the cardboard backing, was a phone number and the name "Ben". He would not have seen the faint printing had it not been for the bright light. Then he noticed, even more obscurely printed, a date -7/26. This opened up a whole new bag of questions. Because of its location, it was apparent this information was not meant to be seen. So why not memorize it and leave no evidence? The answer had to be that Pete wanted it to be found. In case something happened to him, hopefully the right person would find it. It was a reach, but it was all Tony had.

Today was the 26th, and it was already 10:30 p.m. He couldn't use the phone, and he definitely couldn't leave the grounds by car. That would alert them; he might as well send up a red flag. He knew the location of a pay phone nearby, but it was a little too far even if he chose to jog. He remembered a bicycle hanging in his garage. Probably left by a previous tenant. It was risky to say the least. What if he didn't contact this "Ben" until tomorrow? Would it really matter? Maybe he couldn't be contacted at that number if he waited until then.

He talked himself into and out of the idea several times while removing the bicycle from its hangers. The tires were soft, but it was rideable. Before he realized it he was guiding it out the back door. If he crept carefully around the more obscure outer edge of the property toward the gate, he might be able to slip by unnoticed. Maybe Stan would be dozing or reading.

There was a space of about thirty feet between the entrance and dense hedges, well over six feet. Once he was on the main road he could follow the shadows until he was safely out of sight.

He carefully approached the gate, moving silently from shadow to shadow. He could see Stan's face but couldn't tell if his eyes were open or closed. Tony really couldn't afford to get any closer for fear of being detected. Somehow he had to get to the front edge of the shrubbery and dart around it unnoticed. It would be a fairly simple matter without the bicycle, but it was a necessity. He had to go through a large Metropark that bordered the north end of the property. It was at least three or four miles of twisting parkway to a pay phone. The other direction was much shorter, but it would be impossible to go unnoticed even at this late hour. He could not afford to take a gamble. By following the all-purpose path paralleling the parkway, he could definitely avoid being seen. Returning would not be a problem. He could simply hide the bike at the edge of the woods and glide in unnoticed.

As he crouched in the shadows waiting for an opportunity, a car turned into the drive and headed toward the gate. Stan was definitely awake now. The car reached the gate, and what Tony saw made him withdraw further into the shadows. He shivered as he noticed the same black station wagon and that the guard was not Stan, but Joseph.

Fortunately, Tony regained his composure in time to take advantage of the activity at the gate. The passengers of the car and the guard seemed to be engaged in an animated conversation. It had to be now or never. He took a deep breath and prayed his movement would go undetected.

He moved quickly around the corner of the hedge and passed unseen into the haven of darkness. He heaved a sigh of relief as the blackness swallowed him up. After a reasonably safe distance, he hopped on the bicycle and began peddling furiously. The bike path was totally in shadows and made continuing at high speed hazardous. Branches were slapping at him from all directions, striking every part of his body. He decided to risk detection and proceed on the road. His adrenaline was pumping energy throughout his body so rapidly he literally flew over the necessary distance.

There ahead, under a dim lamp, was the pay phone. His spirits soared as he quickly dismounted, burst into the booth and began frantically dialing the number. The perspiration soaked his clothing, stinging his eyes and all the scratches he had acquired. The phone began ringing one, two, three, four times. He heard a click, then a recorded message.

"We're sorry but that number has been disconnected."

Tony sank to the floor. He sat there several minutes pondering his options. Actually, there were none. He sluggishly rose and began riding back toward the gate. His mind was so focused on his dilemma the gate appeared before he could react. No one saw him, however, and he was able to fade into the shadows around the hedge to safety.

Exhausted, he flopped on his bed, fully clothed. Although his mind was exploding with unanswered questions, fatigue took over and he fell asleep.

———◦———

A loud pounding on his door awakened him. "Tony, it's 8:00 a.m., and you're needed at the office in ten minutes." The voice was Joe, one of the drivers. "You'd better get your rear in gear; they don't look too happy."

Tony flew out of bed, his heart racing. He'd never moved as fast except for possibly the previous night. Somehow he managed to arrive at the office almost within the allotted ten minutes. He took a deep breath, knocked and entered. Carlo Bonitto was seated at his desk facing the windows. Even seated with his back to him, he looked threatening.

Carlo whirled around and rose. Tony felt himself stepping back slightly, anticipating the worst.

"We're glad you could tear yourself away from other more pressing duties," said Bonitto. There was no trace of humor in his voice. "We thought you'd like to meet our new apprentice. Anthony Amico, meet John Libertini." Tony was relieved to know that the reason for his summons was quite innocent.

"Glad to meet you, John."

"Likewise," said Libertini, flashing a toothy grin. "I'm looking forward to my apprenticeship here and working with you, Tony."

"I'm sure we'll make a good team. I'll do everything I can to help you get your feet wet," said Tony, as he closely scrutinized his new partner. His appearance couldn't help but make Tony feel something was wrong with the whole picture.

John was about his size and age, but there the similarity ended. To describe his outfit as tacky was being charitable. In an organization that prided itself on class in manner and dress, he was clearly a deviation. He looked like he'd cornered the gold market. Not only was there a profusion of the stuff, it was gaudy and in the wrong places. His pinkie ring belonged on the hand of someone twice his size, and the gold chains were so bright Tony thought he needed sunglasses to look at them. John's black polo shirt was unbuttoned which only emphasized the tasteless display. He wore no socks, and his feet were squeezed into designer shoes with toes that came to a point. In short, he definitely did not fit the mold of a dignified employee of Good Shepherd. He looked like he just stepped off the set of "Saturday Night Fever."

"Excellent," said Bonitto. "I'm sure John will benefit greatly from your experience. We'll have him work with you for the rest of the week, but first I want him to meet Joshua. He'll catch up with you at lunch."

Tony left the office and headed for the prep room. He hoped no one had noticed the beads of perspiration on his forehead. He was fairly certain it would go undetected by the occupant of the prep room.

For the remainder of the week Tony and John spent a great deal of time together as John was given the usual crash course. Tony remembered how overwhelmed he had felt, especially for the first few days. It seemed strange to him that John didn't exhibit the same frustrations. Equally strange were John's interest in Pete and his relationship with Tony. Though the attempt was subtle, he detected a more-than-casual interest.

"If this guy's an apprentice, then I'm Frank Sinatra," thought Tony as he went along with the charade. "If I can convince this joker our relationship had been purely professional, maybe their suspicions will go away. It might help buy more time until I figure out who 'Ben' is and whether he knows anything."

Saying John was not his type was an understatement. He epitomized all the traits that Tony disliked. He was loud, profane, boastful, a real know-it-all. Tony would have to work awfully hard to just tolerate him.

For the remainder of the week Tony played their game. If John was going to provide Bonitto with any vital information, it wasn't going to come from him.

To his relief, after that first week Tony's contact with John was reduced. He made no effort to extend their relationship beyond a strictly professional level. The less he saw of John the better he liked it. John would occasionally ask him to go out after work. When he couldn't come up with a satisfactory excuse, they would go out for a few beers. No matter how aggressively John probed (subtlety was not his strong suit), Tony chose his words and answers carefully to deflect more questions.

Tony would sit and listen to John's arrogant boasting. It didn't matter what subject happened to come up. John had "been there and done that." He constantly fought the temptation to tell John what he really thought of him. Realizing this would be a tactical blunder he bit his tongue and never let his responses go beyond casual small talk. "If they are trying to use John to get information from me, they're wasting their time," he thought. "How could they entrust anything of importance to this loser?"

John never volunteered anything about his personal life other than that he grew up in the area and attended Ohio State. As little as John had been able to detect, Tony learned even less about John. The relationship was uneasy as both men tried to conceal it in an attempt not to reveal their true motives. Tony had concluded that John was definitely not an apprentice. He was working for Good Shepherd, but in what capacity remained unknown.

The final tip-off came one day when they were preparing a rather large, elderly woman for viewing that evening. As they were easing her into the casket, Tony lost his grip and almost dropped her.

John blurted out angrily, "You're lucky she didn't fall on the floor. Uncle Carlo would've had your ass."

Tony pretended to be totally concentrating on repositioning the deceased in the casket. In spite of the strange expression on John's face, Tony looked at him blankly. He gave no indication that his blunder had registered.

"I almost lost her, John, but she looks O.K. now. That was a close call." He continued, hoping to deflect any further concerns John may have had. "I guess we're finished here. I think I'll catch some supper. Care to join me?"

"I've got a date for dinner tonight," responded John in a rather subdued voice.

Tony's suspicions were now irrevocably confirmed. There was now no doubt about his purpose in being paired with John. His back was up against the wall with absolutely no one to turn to.

He was definitely beginning to feel like a prisoner. The phone was bugged, and John was a phony. Whenever he left the grounds, John accompanied him. Tony was getting more uptight with every passing day. Hiding what he felt and knew (which wasn't much) was a tremendous strain. He questioned his motives for continuing the charade. He missed the one person who could relieve his anxieties as well as shed light on questions that were slowly eroding his sanity. He had to do something before he made a mistake that could cost him his life. He was certain the only thing preventing him from sharing Pete's fate was the fact he was "family."

Maybe that was his answer - he needed to talk to Uncle Gino. And soon. It was time to take another bicycle ride.

———————

It was easier getting to the pay phone the second time. As he put in money and dialed, he prayed Uncle Gino would be home, and that Mama wouldn't.

He was in luck. Gino answered on the third ring.

"Uncle Gino, it's Tony. I need to talk to you. But not if Mama's home. Is she?"

"No, she went to St. Joan's to Mass. What can I do for you?" asked Uncle Gino.

"I had a friend, Pete, who came home with me at Blossom Time. He's disappeared. Before he did, he told me there were things going on at Good Shepherd that he was investigating. He was going to tell me everything, but before he could, he vanished."

Gino's voice quivered. "I knew this was a big mistake from the beginning. I was afraid this would happen. Now you're into matters that you have no business being in. Tell me how I can help."

The words tumbled out. "I guess I'm trying to figure out if my godfather is behind whatever is going on, or is it Carlo Bonitto? He's a particularly cold person; one I think could kill someone and never bat an eye! It wouldn't make me feel bad if he were to go to prison and I had something to do with it. But how can I do that to my godfather after everything he's done for me? But what if he did order Pete killed? Should I keep looking for evidence? What if he gets caught because of me? How can I reconcile what I'm trying to do with family loyalty? Would that be honorable? That's what my dad wouldn't have done. But I'm not my dad." Tony stopped speaking long enough to catch his breath.

Gino took advantage of the break. "Tony, I can't tell you what to do. The only advice I can give you is to follow your instincts. Follow what your heart tells your head, not the other way around. If I could do this for you, I would. This you have to decide for yourself. And then live with it."

"I guess what you mean is I have to decide which matters most - loyalty, family, obligation, honor, respect or right and wrong. Or some combination?" asked Tony. This was heavy stuff, and he was on the proverbial horns of a dilemma.

"That's exactly what I mean. And only you can answer that question. I will tell you one additional bit of information that might make your decision easier. You are right - Bonitto is truly an evil man. I can't say that about your father and godfather. So you decide. What does count most?" Gino finished.

"Thanks, Uncle Gino. You're such a wise man. I almost knew what you would tell me before I asked. I want you to know how much you mean to me. I've got to go now. Wish me luck." Tony rang off, retrieved his bicycle, and headed back to Good Shepherd.

Still holding the phone to his ear, Gino sat staring at the family portrait directly in front of him. Would those happy smiling faces ever be the same again? Gino didn't know the answer. His eyes welled up and tears began to trickle down his cheeks.

15

Tony's only other clue was from a brief conversation he had had with Pete concerning Terri. Locating her and avoiding detection would require skill far beyond his abilities. He knew only her first name and that she had recently moved to Toledo from somewhere on the West Side. Terri was to take a position as a hostess in an upscale Italian restaurant.

"Not much to go on," he thought. "Where in the hell do I begin?" Somehow he had to get to Toledo and find an Italian restaurant that had just hired a hostess named Terri. "A piece of cake," he scoffed, "if your name is Sherlock Holmes."

His first problem was getting to Toledo without drawing suspicion. He had to come up with a plan. It finally came to him like a bolt out of the blue. He would tell them that he needed to attend a friend's wedding in Philadelphia. Someone on the staff could drive him to the airport where he would enter the terminal under the pretext of boarding a plane. He would rent a car instead, drive to Toledo and begin his sleuthing.

"Sounds almost too simple," he thought. "That probably means it is. I'm not giving these guys much credit." Since he couldn't use the phone, he decided to write Uncle Gino and explain what he planned to do. If they called to check on him, Uncle Gino would confirm his story. That evening he mailed the letter. He would ask Carlo for permission to go to the "wedding" in the morning.

Tony had a sleepless night thinking of all the possible scenarios. By morning he had carefully mapped out every detail of his story. Even so, he did not feel particularly confident regarding his ability to convince Bonitto of his sincerity. Summoning his nerve, he knocked on the office door. It opened immediately. There, face to face, was the menacing figure of Carlo Bonitto. Tony could almost feel his hot breath in his face as he spoke.

"Come in and sit down, Tony," commanded Carlo. "I understand you have a request." Bonitto always liked to stand while talking to employees. It gave him a feeling of control - as if he needed more.

"I've been invited to a friend's wedding next Saturday in Philadelphia," he lied. "I could fly there on Friday, attend the wedding and be back by Sunday. If I fly, I'll miss as little work as possible," he explained.

"Sounds like you have everything pretty well thought out," said Bonitto, looking at Tony with eyes that seemed to see right through him. Tony held his breath and waited for whatever was to come next. To his relief, Bonitto flashed what might be interpreted as a slight smile.

"By all means, Tony, we try to do anything we can to accommodate employee's requests. I will have John drive you to the airport and pick you up if you will inform him of the times. Was there anything else you wished to discuss?"

"Nothing," said Tony. "Thanks for giving me the time off." He left the office feeling relief the first part had gone according to plan.

For the next five days Tony was convinced all eyes were scrutinizing his every move. He had to keep reassuring himself it was just his imagination.

After what seemed like an eternity, the day finally arrived. He was packed and ready an hour before John was to pick him up. The time couldn't go fast enough. Then he heard it - the horn announcing John's arrival. He rushed out, threw his luggage in the back seat and got in. John gave a grunt of acknowledgment and they were off. It was only a forty-minute drive, but it seemed much longer due to the tension between the two men. Few words were spoken, and both were relieved as John pulled into the Continental Airlines departure zone.

"Thanks John. See you Sunday at 4:30," said Tony. He could swear he heard John mumble, "And good riddance."

Pausing at the entrance long enough to see John drive off, he rushed to the escalator. Descending to the lower level, he made his way to the Alamo car rental counter. About fifteen minutes later he was on the road for the three-hour ride to Toledo.

———

The cell phone rang. "Hello, who's this?" asked John.

"Who do you think it is, you idiot," hissed Bonitto. "I got tired of waiting to hear what happened. Did you see our boy off?"

"Well, not exactly," said Libertini haltingly. "Doesn't he think I can do anything right?" he murmured under his breath.

"And just what is that supposed to mean?" asked Carlo trying to control himself.

"Well, I dropped him off, and now I'm heading back."

"You mean you didn't stay long enough to watch him board?" bellowed Carlo, no longer able to control himself. "Did it ever occur to you that he might not have even boarded?"

"No, it didn't, Uncle Carlo," John responded meekly.

"Turn around and get back there," Bonitto said as his voice started rising again. "Go to the desk and make sure he actually boarded, then call me immediately." He was now ranting.

"Yes, Uncle Carlo," John said, holding the phone about a foot from his ear. Then the phone went dead.

"I'm tired of taking his crap. One of these days I'm not going to take it any longer and he'll be sorry," said

John bravely as he threw the phone down on the seat.

⟡

Tony wasn't sure how to tackle the problem of locating Terri. Unless he got lucky, he could spend the major part of his time attempting to locate her. Then he needed time to talk to her to find out what she knew. It was a long shot to assume she even knew anything. He had no clue how intimate she and Pete had been. Why should she even trust him anyway? He'd come this far so he'd have to play the scene to its conclusion.

As he drove west on the Turnpike, he couldn't help but think of the proverbial "needle-in-the-haystack"

⟡

John swaggered up to the departure desk. The attendant was talking to an associate, but that didn't stop John. "Can I get some help here? I'm in a hurry."

The attendant looked at him. Whatever she was thinking, she still forced a smile. "How can we help you, sir?"

"My brother left some important papers, and I need to get them to him," said John, impressed by his craftiness. "I'm not sure which flight he is on. Can you tell me if a Tony Amico left on flight number 1481 for Philadelphia?"

"I'll be happy to check our list if you'll give me a moment."

John paced impatiently in front of the counter. "I'm sorry, sir, but he did not make the flight. Is there..."

Libertini turned in the middle of her sentence and rushed from the counter to the pay phone across the concourse. He would have to swallow his pride again and tell Uncle Carlo of this recent development.

"Nice job," Carlo replied coldly. "It's a good thing you're my nephew although sometimes I hate to admit it. Our only other option is to check the car rentals. But if he left on the rapid transit, taxi, or some other way, we're out of luck. Get downstairs and check it out. For your sake I hope you come up with something," Carlo warned him.

The nearest car rental adjacent to the escalator was Alamo. Libertini surprisingly reasoned he might stop there first. "Excuse me," he said a little more tactfully. "My brother left some important papers. I need to find him as soon as possible. His name is Tony Amico. If you could check your records, I'd appreciate it."

"I'll check for you, sir," said the attendant, punching some keys on the computer. "Yes, here it is," he announced. "He left about twenty minutes ago. His destination appears to be Toledo."

Libertini turned without a word, walked to the nearest phone and dialed excitedly. "Uncle Carlo," he proudly announced, "he rented from Alamo, and he's headed for Toledo."

"Good work," said Uncle Carlo. "I'm proud of you. Give me the make, color and license number and we'll take it from there."

In his excitement John hadn't thought to get the information from the clerk. He swallowed hard and told Uncle Carlo.

"You never cease to amaze me. Keep our connection and go back to Alamo. This time be sure to ask for everything."

Libertini ran over to the counter and practically begged for the information Bonitto had demanded. He returned to the phone, and breathing hard, announced, "Ford Taurus, Red, LOB7171."

"Thanks so much. Now try to find your way back here without getting lost," Bonitto said. He slammed the phone down so hard Libertini recoiled from the sound.

16

When Tony reached the city limits, he began looking for a phone. He figured the yellow pages were the best place to start. Not necessarily the best plan, but the only one he had. He pulled into a truck stop and found a phone book that was in reasonably good condition. Under "restaurants" he found two pages of names. Looking disheartedly at a list half as long as his arm, he went to the cashier and bought three rolls of quarters.

After an hour and a half, his patience exhausted, Tony slumped into a booth and rested his head on the table.

"Can't sleep in here, friend," a hard-bitten waitress said as she slapped her hand on the table right next to his ear.

Tony's head shot up with his eyes wide open. "I'm sorry," he said, "I just can't stay awake any longer."

"Don't need to apologize, friend; I just follow orders here. If you need a place to sleep, there's a cheap motel out back. I wouldn't go out on the road if I was you."

"Thanks for the advice. I think I'll take it," said Tony with a weary smile. "No sense beating a dead horse. Most of the restaurants are closed by now anyway. I'll get a fresh start in the morning."

A short time later he collapsed into a lumpy bed. Too mentally exhausted to contemplate the task ahead, he fell asleep immediately.

He awoke with a start. The noise of the day served as his wake-up call long before the alarm went off. He showered, shaved, dressed and left the shabby room with renewed vitality. After a hearty breakfast, he went back to the pay phone. It was around 11:15 when he connected with "A Little Bite of Italy" and hit the jackpot. Terri wouldn't be in until 3:00, and policy prevented them from giving out any personal information. He got directions to the restaurant, got in his car and went to find "A Little Bite of Italy."

After he had located it, he drove downtown to see the new Center of Science and Industry on the site of the old Portside project. Tony bought a ticket and walked around for awhile. It had a great view of the River. He stopped to get a sandwich and a soda. By then it was time to head back. He got back in his car and drove to the restaurant.

He entered the restaurant about three and nervously waited for Terri to show up. The establishment was not overly large, but it truly was upscale. Everyone was busy preparing for the evening's business. It was bedecked in the traditional Italian style, and celebrity photographs decorating the wall proclaimed its status. He sat sipping a glass of Chianti, taking in the scene. "If I owned a restaurant," he mused, "I'd want it to be just like this."

Just then a young woman entered carrying a stack of menus. She was tall, slender and quite attractive. Her short skirt accentuated long shapely legs that made her seem even taller. Her dark hair had a beautiful sheen to it. Tony couldn't decide whether it was her legs or her hair that were more impressive. In any event, Pete deserved credit for having excellent taste.

As he walked toward her, she sensed he wanted to talk to her. Accustomed to being "hit on" by members of the opposite sex, she pretended to be distracted, turned her back to him and began moving away.

Tony was so intent on his purpose that he didn't even notice her rebuff. He pleaded, "Please, Terri, I must have a word with you." She whirled at the sound of her name and looked at him with a wary frown.

"Well, what is it? I'm very busy," she said impatiently.

"I'm a friend of Pete Boggio. I need to talk to you."

She looked shocked. She grabbed him by the arm and ushered him into a small checkroom.

"What do you know about Pete? Where is he?" she demanded. "I haven't heard from him in a month." She was frantic, but she was also suspicious. "How did you find me?"

"My name is Tony Amico. I worked with Pete at Good Shepherd. He and I were becoming good friends when he just disappeared. No one knows what happened to him. He had told me about you so I came here to find you and see what you might know."

She slumped against the wall as tears began to flow. "I was afraid of this," she sobbed. "I told him to get out of there. He said he was almost finished with what he had to do. I knew something was terribly wrong. There were times he told me he feared for his life."

"Is there anything else you can tell me?" pleaded Tony. "I need something that will help me find him or find out what happened to him."

"We do need to talk," she said, "but not now. I get off at 10:30 and I'll be home by 11:00. Here's my phone number. Call me, and I'll arrange a place for us to meet. Be careful. We have to assume these people are capable of anything," she said in a barely audible voice.

She turned back to her station without another word. The look of terror on her face made Tony pause. Was he doing the right thing drawing her into this mess? If she could provide some answers, possibly the risk they were both taking was worth it. The nagging question was did it justify jeopardizing his life and that of a beautiful young woman he barely knew?

He walked out of the restaurant. Heeding her warning, he remained in well-lit public places the rest of the day and into the evening. Remembering how much Pete had liked the Cleveland Museum of Art he got directions to the Toledo Museum of Art. He figured he owed Pete that. And it was a good museum. He decided he'd have to go to the Cleveland Museum of Art when this whole situation was resolved.

He got back in his car. Someone at the museum had recommended Shale's Pharmacy, known for their milkshakes and deli food. So he got directions, stopped at Shale's for a late supper and chocolate milkshake, and then looked for a pay phone. At precisely 11:00 he dialed the number she had given him.

"Tony?" It was Terri.

"Yes, are you all right?" he asked.

"I think so, but it would be safer if you came to my place. Where are you now?"

"I'm in a bar at the corner of Hastings and 14th Avenue."

"Good," she said. "You're only about five minutes away. Take Hastings north to 4th Avenue. I live in a small house behind the duplex right on the corner. Please hurry," she pleaded.

He had no trouble following her directions. Parking the car on the main street, he cautiously walked down the narrow, dimly lit alley toward the small house in the rear. His heart was racing as he stepped on the small porch and raised his hand to knock on the screen door. But before he could, someone grabbed him from behind and dragged him off the porch. He struggled, but it was useless. His assailant held him fast. He felt a slight pinch in the back of his neck, and that was the last thing he remembered. Within seconds everything went blank.

———➤•◦•◄———

Tony slowly opened his eyes. For a moment he could not remember anything. As he lay there trying to focus his eyes, he gradually became aware of a tall hedge looming over him. A security light was shining from somewhere behind it. A slight breeze caused the leaves to dance, casting shadows and light in intermittent patterns on his face. He shook his head, and everything slowly began to come into focus. He was lying next to Terri's porch concealed among tall hedges. He struggled to his feet and staggered up to the porch.

It wasn't until then that he realized he was clutching something in his hand. With a look of horror, he let out a gasp and dropped the object on the ground. A sick feeling came over him as he looked down at it. The object was metallic, almost two feet in length and about the diameter of the handle of a baseball bat. It was covered with the black-red color of dried blood.

Stumbling up the steps, he walked through the partially opened door. The sight in the small living room forced him to his knees. Sprawled on the floor was Terri's lifeless body. Her clothing was soaked with dried blood and one side of her head was shattered, exposing splintered bone and brain matter. Her eyes were staring vacantly. Crawling over to her, his hands probed for any sign of life.

A gasp came from behind him. An elderly woman was standing in the doorway. He struggled to his feet and brushed past her. Panic-stricken, he raced through the alley to his car. Fumbling for his keys, he could hear her screaming loudly as she stumbled out of the house. He started the motor and screeched recklessly out into the street. He didn't turn on his headlights. He was hoping against hope that no one could see him clearly enough to make a positive identification.

⸻※◦※⸻

A man dressed in black from head to toe appeared from behind the house. He bent over, and with rubber gloves, carefully picked up the murder weapon, placed it in a plastic bag and disappeared into the shadows.

⸻※◦※⸻

Regaining some degree of composure, Tony felt he was far enough away from the grisly scene to slow down. He didn't want to risk being stopped for reckless driving. As he slowed the car the full horror of what had happened washed over him.

Was he being set up? If so, by whom? Or was he just in the wrong place at the wrong time? Why wasn't he murdered as well? It had to be calculated and not a random act of violence. He assumed his fingerprints were on the murder weapon.

Gradually, as his head cleared, he tried to analyze his predicament. No one from the funeral home could have known he was in Toledo. There couldn't be a connection. They thought he was in Philadelphia. Uncle Gino would verify it if they checked. But was he giving them enough credit? They were far more experienced at this cat-and-mouse game than he had ever wished to be. There were just too many coincidences. He had to assume that somehow they knew his every move.

Fighting back tears, he thought of poor innocent Terri. Maybe she'd be alive if it weren't for him. He would never forgive himself if her death were the result of him involving her in this mess. Thinking back, he recalled John and Josh had both expressed an interest in her. Could they have followed him? Had he led them to her and caused her death? In his mind his debt to Pete, justified or not, had now taken on an additional dimension. He was determined to find out one way or another.

—————⟫•◦•⟪—————

The sun was just coming up as he approached a service plaza. He pulled in and went directly to the washroom. He needed to shave and clean up. Food was not a factor at this point. Other events were still too fresh in his mind. The murder of Terri kept him in a constant state of shock. He found himself fighting back tears each time the scene materialized.

Back on the road, he began attacking the problem of his own survival. What if Libertini were waiting for him at the gate when he was supposed to arrive from Philadelphia? That was a distinct possibility. How could he explain not being on the plane? Chances were John would be waiting in the car unless he had been told otherwise. Tony decided to get to the terminal early. He could explain it had been more convenient for his friends to get him to the airport earlier than anticipated. Instead of sitting around for half a day, he had taken an earlier flight. If they thought he was actually in Philly, they'd buy it. If they knew where he really had been, it didn't matter anyway.

He sat and waited nervously in the terminal. To his relief, there was no sign of John Libertini as the passengers from Philly disembarked. There was no guarantee that some other "wiseguy" was not there watching. He slowly walked out to the curb at the arrival zone. A honk informed him of Libertini's presence.

As Tony hopped in he was greeted with "I sure hope you had a good time. We were busy as hell while you were gone," in a voice oozing with sarcasm.

"I'll bet you were, you son-of-a-bitch," thought Tony. "Sorry, John, I guess you never know in our business."

"Yeah," he remarked, "I always said if business is slow, plan a trip and you'll get a death call within the hour."

"Right you are," said Tony. "There's more truth to that than you can possibly know,' thought Tony as he fought back another flood of guilt-laden tears.

That was the extent of their conversation except for a few probing questions by John. Tony was noncommittal. There was little exchange during the remainder of the trip.

Exhausted, Tony finally reached his room. The nervous energy that had carried him through the last two days had abandoned him. He fell on his bed, fully clothed, and never stirred again until the alarm woke him at 7:00 the following morning.

17

It had been over a month since Pete had vanished. Other than the appearance of John, there was nothing out of the ordinary. But the tension was definitely taking its toll. Besides the constant pressure of wondering what Bonitto and his henchmen were plotting, he had the ill-fated trip to Toledo preying on his mind. No matter how hard he tried, the image of Terri's bloody corpse occupied his thoughts constantly. The guilt he felt became over-whelming at times. His only release came when he was preoccupied with a task at work. And those moments were becoming increasingly rare. His sleep was fitful and his appetite was nonexistent. He was losing weight. It had to be obvious to everyone that something was bother-ing him.

He needed to get away for awhile. Nighttown was an option, even though his association with the local nightspot was not a happy one. Desperation, along with his limited knowledge of the area, narrowed his options so he headed to Nighttown grudgingly. However, leaving the grounds had immediately buoyed his spirits. By the time he pulled into the parking lot, Tony was whistling along with a tune on the radio. He was feeling better and look-ing forward to a few well-earned hours of parole.

As he seated himself, he couldn't help but notice an attractive young woman working behind the bar. There was something familiar about her, but he quickly dis-missed the idea. However, when he chanced to look up, their eyes met. She smiled as she approached him.

"What'll you have, Tony," she said in a soft, sultry voice. His jaw dropped open, which prompted a giggle.

"I'll bet you're wondering how I know your name." She pointed a well-manicured nail at his chest. Tony's face flushed as he realized the reason. In his haste to leave, he had failed to remove his identification tag.

Regaining his composure he responded, "Nuts, I thought we knew each other. I guess I'm not that lucky."

She smiled brightly and extended her long slender hand toward his. "Well then, it's only fair that I tell you my name."

"Only fair," said Tony eagerly as he grasped her hand.

"I'm Carley Benton; glad to meet you, Tony." She hesitated, waiting for his response.

He quickly regained what little composure he possessed.

"Tony, Tony Amico," he finally sputtered, "and the pleasure is all mine."

"What can I get you, Tony Amico?" she asked with more than casual interest in her voice.

"I'll have a Crooked River draft and a bag of those peanuts," he said in his most cool voice. As luck would have it, the bar was practically deserted so he had her virtually to himself. "What incredible good fortune; don't blow it, you klutz," he thought.

She was almost as tall as he was, slender and flat-out gorgeous. She would look more at home on the cover of Cosmopolitan than serving drinks at Nighttown.

Returning with his drink, she pushed the money back at him. "I'm new on the job. The first one's on me. That way you'll have to come back." Tony grinned. It felt strange since he hadn't smiled in weeks.

"You don't have to worry about that; you could have charged me double, and I'd be back." He surprised himself with the ease at which he threw out the line.

She smiled at his clumsy attempt at being cool. "Where do you go when you wear that name tag, Tony Amico?"

"I'm an apprentice at Good Shepherd Funeral Home. This is my first year." Just as he started to say more, a look came over her face that made Tony feel like he had just told her he was a serial killer. Her shoulders slumped and her head dropped. She was shaking and began to sob quietly.

"Carley, what's wrong?" he asked.

She quickly controlled herself and looked deeply into his eyes. "It's not your fault, Tony. That place has made my life unbearable. I hope you won't mind my burdening you. This kind of talk usually comes from the opposite side of the bar." She continued, and what she said next made Tony blink in disbelief.

"My sister's boyfriend worked there until he disappeared without a trace about a month ago. Shortly after that, my only sister was found murdered in Toledo. I know their deaths are related. I took this job knowing it was popular with the employees of Good Shepherd. I know I'm grasping at straws, but I have no other options. I have to find out what happened. I won't rest until I do. I know that you knew Pete. Did you know my sister, Terri?"

Tony was dumbfounded. He couldn't believe what he was hearing.

"Tony, are you all right? This has to be quite a shock, meeting me here like this. I was praying you would come in soon."

He realized that he had not responded to her question. "I'm sorry, I was so taken back by what you said. Yes, I knew Pete pretty well, but I never had the pleasure of meeting your sister." Though it was not in his nature to lie, he just couldn't bring himself to tell her the truth. At least not yet. It would be impossible to explain his meeting with Terri and the circumstances surrounding her death. It could have been pure coincidence, but he didn't rule out the possibility of a connection with Good Shepherd. He definitely shared her suspicions but suppressed the desire to spill it all out right then and there.

Carley continued. "It's just too bizarre. Don't you think it's more than just a little bit strange?"

Tony continued his deception. "It's hard to say, Carley. Nothing has come to light how and why Pete disappeared. Did the Toledo police give you anything to go on?"

"Nothing," Carley responded with a tone of disgust. "It's as if she never existed and nothing ever happened - just another unsolved homicide. I've reached the point where I feel that if anything is ever going to be discovered in this whole mess, I'm going to have to do my own detective work."

Tony protested. "You can't be serious. If the professionals can't discover anything, how in the world do you think you can?" As soon as he blurted the words out, he wished he could grab them and stuff them back in his big mouth.

"Now you sound like everyone else. Give me a little credit," she snapped back at him. "I know more about Good Shepherd than you might think, and so did Terri. There's got to be a connection."

"If you believe what you are saying, why are you telling me, a perfect stranger? Assuming Terri knew too much and was murdered, isn't that a little risky?"

Carley agreed. "Under normal circumstances, it would be about the stupidest thing I've ever done in my life. Terri told me things that Pete had confided to her. I guess we were all pretty naive regarding the dangers involved. We just couldn't understand how people could kill others without batting an eye. We thought that stuff was just part of the make-believe world of movies and TV. Anyway, Pete had mentioned a fellow worker who was the only person in the place he could trust. He called him 'Tony' and felt confident enough to ask him to help. That was just before Pete disappeared. So I came here looking for the only person in the world I thought could help. I had no idea how I'd find this Tony or make contact, much less get him to help me. I'm lucky you came in here tonight. I knew right away you were the one Pete had talked about. He was very fond of you, and I can see why." Tony felt his face getting hot.

She looked at him pleadingly and squeezed his hand tightly. "You will help me, won't you?"

Though the bar separated them, her face was so close he could smell her perfume. He thought she was the most beautiful creature he'd ever seen. He could feel his heart pounding as he searched for just the right words.

"Carley, if what you believe is true, then two people are already dead because of that information. If they discover your identity and what you're up to, they won't hesitate to make it three. I know nothing at this point, but if you promise to keep a low profile and leave the snooping up to me, I'll see what I can find out. Please promise to be patient and let me do the detective work. I'll fill you in on everything. Besides, that will give me a good excuse to see you."

Her arms reached across the bar. She clasped her hands behind his neck and pulled him toward her. Her lips brushed his lightly as she spoke.

"Thank you, Tony," she whispered. "You don't need any excuse to see me, and I do hope it will be often." She released her grip, and Tony almost fell backward off the barstool. She giggled as he awkwardly regained his balance.

Tony hoped that no one had noticed the intimate conversation. To his relief, the bar was empty. He knew they would have to be more cautious in the future. He cleared his throat and tried to sound in control. If she sensed he had completely gone bonkers over her, she didn't let on. She continued to look longingly into his eyes as he tried to speak intelligently.

"Carley, you can't phone me, and I can't phone you. I know I'm being closely watched and my phone is tapped. What's your work schedule?"

"I work weekdays till closing. I'm off on weekends. That could change since this is only my second week on the job."

Suddenly they were back to the reality of a dangerous situation. There would be time for other things later. Survival was now the main agenda.

"I'd better get back," he said as he tenderly brushed the hair across her forehead and slid his hand down the side of her face. She turned her head slightly and pressed her lips into the palm of his hand.

"Hurry back, Tony Amico," she purred as he turned and made his way out of the bar. Leaving took all the will power he could muster, but he knew their safety depended on discretion.

He didn't even remember walking to the car. It was most likely because his feet probably never touched the ground. Getting into his car, he began to worry. "What a dilemma," he thought. "I've met the most incredible woman I've ever known, and if I see her as much as I'd like, she could end up in a body bag. I still can't believe she would stick her pretty neck out like that with a perfect stranger. I really must have an honest face," he reasoned. "I'm not going to question her motives." He had mixed emotions about the whole situation, but the electricity he had felt was not to be denied.

He was so preoccupied that he didn't notice the familiar black station wagon pulling out of the parking lot as he left. It wasn't until he turned onto the road entering the grounds that he noticed he'd been followed.

He shivered as he realized his lack of caution and the potential danger that still lurked. He had acted with his heart and not his head. He couldn't afford to allow that to happen again. He had assumed the responsibility for another person - one he definitely did not want to lose.

Suddenly life had become even more complex. Any possible thoughts he had about leaving and blowing the whole thing off had taken on a new direction. The lovely Carley had complicated an already impossible situation.

Wednesday morning was gloomy and rainy - a perfect backdrop for Tony's dilemma. He was assigned to drive a limo for a family whose elderly father had died. The cortege would proceed from Good Shepherd, where the funeral took place, to All Souls Cemetery in Chardon for committal. Tony was waiting with the limousine as the family appeared.

As he held the door of the limo, a middle-aged man got in and looked at Tony intently as though he wanted to say something. There was no mistaking the deliberate eye contact. Tony continued to watch the man closely through the rear view mirror for any further signs of communication. He saw nothing unusual for the remainder of the day and decided it was just another case of overblown paranoia. His mind vacillated between the previous night's encounter with the girl of his dreams, the potential peril they both shared and the mysterious man in the back seat of the limo. He didn't even recall the drive back.

When they returned to the funeral home, Tony opened the door for the family to exit. The man handed him a twenty-dollar tip and thanked him for his services. Though he watched, Tony saw no sign of recognition. Tony accepted the tip and thanked him in return.

In the process of unfolding the bill to put in his wallet, he noticed a piece of paper attached to the underside. He quickly refolded the money and placed it in his pocket. To his relief, no one had noticed this exchange. He would look at the paper later in the privacy of his room.

After what seemed like an eternity, Tony excitedly entered his apartment and locked the door behind him.

He figured the safest place would be in the bathroom. At this point there was no such thing as being overly cautious.

He reached in his pocket and, with trembling hands, unfolded the twenty-dollar bill exposing the small piece of paper. Something was faintly written on one side. He held it close to the light. What he saw sent a chill up and down his body, but it was also coupled with an extreme sense of relief.

⟩•◦•⟨

Thursday , 8:30 p.m., Nightttown!

Thursday evening finally arrived. Another day of waiting and Tony feared he would lose what little sanity he had left. As he approached the gate, he was relieved to see Stan's friendly face.

"Taking in a movie at the Centrum; I hope they won't need me. If they do, just tell them you never saw me. I must have snuck by you."

"Things seem pretty slow, but you never know in this business," retorted Stan. "I hear they're dying to get in here."

"Boy, that's a new one, Stan; who writes your material?" joked Tony. "Keep the light on for me," he yelled as he pulled out. His stomach felt like it did on a first date. In weeks filled with anxieties, this was right up there with the most unnerving he had experienced. Adding Carley to the mix pushed the scenario almost beyond comprehension. He still hadn't figured out how he was going to appease Carley. He had to protect her at all cost.

By the time he pulled into Nighttown's parking lot, he felt slightly less panicky. He entered the restaurant and headed for the bar, his eyes nervously shifting from person to person. Then he saw Carley. The man who had passed him the note was not there. Tony sat at the corner of the bar facing the door as Carley approached him, smiling.

"What'll it be sailor?" she asked jokingly.

He smiled nervously, and she immediately knew something was wrong.

"Don't laugh, but I'll just have a club soda with a twist."

"Whatever you say. Are you O.K.?"

"I'm fine," he lied, but there was no concealing his nervousness. "I had a super stressful day and just need to relax."

"I wish I could jump over this bar and hold you," she whispered. "As you can see, we're really busy so I'll have to put that fantasy on hold for now."

It was almost 8:30 when the front door opened. Tony's heart sank as John Libertini strutted in with a young lady on his arm. He held his breath and lowered his head. After a moment he slowly looked up, relieved to see Libertini heading into the dining area. Tony ordered another club soda and continued his vigil. His nerves were frazzled. He could not keep his hand from shaking as he raised the glass to his lips. His eyes alternated from Carley to the dining room to the bar and a possible contact. Nothing. He was relieved that Carley was busy and only came by occasionally. She was continually looking his way, and her frustration showed clearly. Her pretty face was creased with worry.

Another half-hour passed and still no contact was made. Maybe Libertini's appearance had scared the contact off.

After another half-hour and two more drinks, he decided it was futile to wait any longer. This was all his nerves could endure. Tony was feeling the effect of too many club sodas so he headed for the restroom near the end of the bar.

As Tony entered, a man brushed past him. The man looked him in the eye and whispered, "first stall." Tony turned to get a good look at him, but the man had disappeared into the crowd.

Following the stranger's directions, Tony entered the

stall. No clues here. A dead end!

Just then he heard someone enter the restroom and go into the stall next to him. A scraping noise on the floor attracted his attention, and he looked down at a sight that made him gasp. At his feet was a snub-nosed pistol with a coiled note stuffed through the trigger guard. He picked up the gun and slumped down on the toilet seat. He didn't think his legs could support him. His hands were trembling so badly he could hardly unroll the paper. When he finally focused on the note, its message clearly told him all his concerns had not been groundless.

Tony - Pete told us we could trust you; we need your help badly. We realize we are asking you to involve yourself in something potentially dangerous with very little information. Keep the gun with you at all times. Hopefully you won't have to use it. All exchanges of information will take place in this manner. Whenever you enter the bar, someone will be contacted. Within a half-hour, enter this stall. Since Pete's disappearance, you are our only source of help. Never let your guard down. These people are extremely dangerous and have no regard for human life. Stay alert - your life may depend on it. I know you have many questions, and we will provide you with answers soon. I hope you will help us put some very high-profile criminals away for good.
--Special Agent Ben Griffin, FBI.

Tony wondered what they wanted from him. Did he want to risk his life to find out? He'd never fired a gun in his life. He guessed he knew how, but it was not something he had ever anticipated doing. It would go under his mattress, and then he'd forget about it. All he had to do was never show up at Nighttown again, and maybe they would leave him alone. On the other hand, it was probably too late. Was he willing to commit to whatever cost Pete his life? This was his new predicament that would replace the others causing his sleepless nights. But at least he now knew who the mysterious 'Ben' was from the notepad in Pete's apartment.

As he walked out of the restroom, one thing was certain - the danger was real. If he involved Carley further, her life would be in danger, too. He could not allow this to happen. He would not allow this to happen. If she didn't understand and became angry with him, if she never spoke to him again, at least she would still be alive.

He waved to a puzzled Carley as he slowly walked out along the bar. The pained look on his face told her more than any words could. She bit her lower lip and fought back tears as she sensed she might never see him again.

Tony left the bar and trudged dejectedly to the parking lot. He heard a familiar voice frantically calling out his name. He whirled to see Carley rushing toward him. As much as he ached for her, this was the worst possible thing that could happen. She stopped short and looked at him with red-rimmed eyes.

"What happened?" she asked with a pleading voice. "Is it something I've said or done? Don't leave like this; please tell me."

His resistance melted. Caution went out the window. He wrapped his arms around her and pulled her close. He wished they could just get in the car and drive away, never looking back.

With all the will power he possessed, Tony's voice cracked. "You have to trust me. I can't talk about it. Don't make this any more difficult than it is. I beg you to leave it alone. I promise I'll tell you all I know when the time is right." His next sentence was one of the most difficult he ever uttered. "Believe me, Carley, I hate to say this," he lowered his head with his voice barely audible, "but it's best if we don't see each other. I'm truly sorry, but I don't see any other way."

"What do you mean?" she shouted. "Excuse me, but it was my sister who was murdered, not yours. How dare you tell me to butt out. You have no right to treat me like a disinterested party."

Tony grabbed her by both shoulders and gave her a

gentle but firm shake. "You have no idea what you're getting into - I'm not sure I do. I'll tell you this much. We're dealing with people who are dangerous beyond our comprehension. I care about you very much and refuse to expose you to something that could bring us down at the blink of an eye."

She started to speak, but he quickly pressed his fingers to her lips.

Tony continued. "You hardly know me, but I'm single-minded and very stubborn. What I say I mean. If it means you never speak to me again, so be it. I'd rather never see you again if it means you will live to a ripe old age.'

Saying that, he quickly turned and practically sprinted to the car. He forced a look out the rear view mirror. The sight of Carley standing alone in the parking lot nearly broke his heart.

His melancholy was so consuming that he never noticed the black station wagon following at a discreet distance.

19

It had been three days since the encounter in the restroom at Nighttown. Tony had vacillated between going back and not going back so many times that his brain was spinning out of control. He was still haunted by his vision of Terri and Carley, lying side by side in matching coffins. He had to make a decision and stick to it before he lost his mind.

A third alternative would be to quit his job at Good Shepherd and go back to Chagrin Falls or someplace even farther away. This choice, added to the mix, confused him even more. Clearly, Good Shepherd was involved in unlawful activities. All evidence led to that conclusion.

It was now that Tony fully appreciated the value of his disciplined lifestyle. The realization made him thankful he had not followed the path of his peers. If he had, he would surely be dead by now. He had no doubt the self-inflicted discipline developed over the years was not only responsible for keeping him alive, but forcing him to see this nightmare to its conclusion. He truly felt he owed Pete, Terri and now Carley the satisfaction of knowing somehow their terrible misfortune would be avenged. No matter what the price, he was determined to bring closure to this whole tragedy.

The only problem he had was still what that closure would be. He knew that Bonitto was truly a bad person. But how bad remained to be seen. He sincerely hoped that Bonitto was behind everything.

There was one more thing to consider. This was probably the most compelling reason of all. He couldn't believe that he had not considered the possibility of involving his family before now. If they suspected he had passed information to anyone, it was as good as signing his death warrant. And the logical conclusion would point directly at members of his family. Who would they think he had had contact with other than them? The prospect of the ones he loved most being placed in serious jeopardy because of him shed an entirely different slant on the whole issue. The chilling realization of what was now at stake forced him to reevaluate his position.

At least he now understood how his father and god-father could be guilty of killing someone for the sake of their families. But instead of the realization making his decision easier, it made it that much more difficult.

If he went to Nighttown, he would surely be contacted. Then he could hopefully get enough information to make an intelligent decision on his course of action. In his heart of hearts he knew he would be making a big mistake to get involved at all. On the other hand, hadn't the Family been allowed to become so powerful because other people had refused to get involved? The only way he could get the truth was to make another trip to Nighttown. He owed that much to Pete and Terri even at the risk of his own life. It was too late for them, but he was determined not to let Carley experience the same fate. Since Carley didn't work on weekends, he prayed she wouldn't be there. He ached when he thought of her, but a life based on discipline kept him on the task. He refused to weaken in his resolve.

Once he had made the decision, a peace came over him that he hadn't experienced in several weeks. Right or wrong, he had made a choice. He climbed in the car and headed out to get some answers.

At 7:30 p.m. he sat down at the Nighttown bar and ordered a beer that would have no taste whatsoever. To his relief Carley was not there. He briefly allowed himself to wish she had been, but that thought was quickly dismissed. He couldn't afford a lack of concentration for one second.

At 8:10 p.m. he went to the restroom and sat on the toilet in stall number one. His heart was pounding so hard Tony swore he could feel the "lub-dub" echoing throughout the stall.

Minutes passed and the pounding grew louder. Suddenly he stopped breathing, and there was a dead silence. Tony looked down. He'd never heard the man enter, but there was a note lying on the floor. He snatched up the paper and hurriedly opened it.

Tony, thanks for coming; we know this was difficult for you. We hope we can make you realize the importance of your decision. Go to the phone booth on the Metroparkway near the funeral home. We will begin trying to contact you there at 9:00 p.m. We will continue trying every fifteen minutes after that until you answer. You deserve a full explanation, and you will get one. No need to remind you, but please be careful.

He crumpled up the paper and flushed it down the toilet. As he left Nighttown, the night air gave him a sudden chill. It was only then that he realized his body was soaked with perspiration. He shivered as he entered the car and headed for a rendezvous in the Metropark.

═══•◦•═══

The phone rang in Bonitto's office. He quickly brought the receiver to his ear. The high-pitched voice on the other end of the line was even higher than usual.

"Amico just left Nighttown, and we're following at a safe distance. Looks like he's heading back. He didn't speak to anyone and stayed for about forty minutes."

"Did he ever leave the bar while he was there?" asked Bonitto excitedly.

"Went to the crapper once," he answered.

"Did you follow him in?"

"No, we didn't think it was important."

"You fool," breathed Bonitto. "Didn't you think it

possible someone could have contacted him in there?"

"Come to think of it, some guy went in shortly after Amico, but we didn't think..."

"That's just the problem. You didn't think! One more mistake like that and you'll wish you were never born." Bonitto slammed the phone down. A few seconds later he dialed another number. "We think Amico made contact tonight. Do you want us to bring him in?"

"Not yet," answered a voice at the other end of the line. "We need to be sure; after all, he is family. You know I do not have the final word in these matters. Be patient, my friend. I have kept my father appraised of the situation. He has his reasons for not wishing to act prematurely. However, I feel confident he will make a decision soon."

The party at the other end of the line hung up, but Carlo continued sitting at his desk. He looked out of his office window across the dimly lit parking lot, focusing on the crematorium. How he wished he could fire it up, and the sooner the better!

As Tony headed for the parkway, he noticed headlights following some distance back. Was someone following him or was his imagination overly active? He recalled the message warning him to be extra cautious.

Slowing down slightly, the headlights remained the same distance behind him. Now he had another problem to deal with. If he caused "them" to blow their cover, "they" would know he was onto them. By forcing their hand, he would probably realize the same fate as Pete. If he just returned to the funeral home, they would not be sure he was onto anything. That way he could buy some time. But he'd have to forfeit getting his answers. It would just have to wait; he couldn't afford to allow curiosity to replace caution at this point in time.

Just to satisfy his nagging curiosity, he sped up and took an alternative route that required more turns than usual. Just as he suspected, the headlights continued to keep pace. There was no question they were trailing him.

As he pulled into the funeral home, the car drove past and appeared to continue down the road. What Tony could not see was the car stopping as it pulled just past the entrance to the Metropark. He waved to Stan as he passed and headed back to his apartment with as many unanswered questions as when he left. This latest disappointment left him quite depressed.

The man with the high-pitched voice pulled out the cell phone and punched in the number that connected him to a waiting Carlo Bonitto.

"He just pulled into the funeral home," informed Squeeky. "I guess we won't find out anything else tonight. What should we do next?"

"Do you think he noticed you following him?" asked Bonitto.

"Not a chance; we stayed far enough back so he could never guess we were on his tail."

"That's strange," snapped Bonitto. "He signed out to go to the movies, went to a bar instead and then came right back here. Don't you find that a little unusual? I won't wait for your answer because it will only upset me more than I already am."

The two men in the car slouched down in their seats as if Bonitto were standing over them and glaring down.

"I want you to turn the car around and remain there until dawn in case he slips out. If either of you dares to close your eyes, I'll pinch your heads off.' He slammed the phone down and rose to look out the window.

As Tony pulled into the garage, he could sense dark sinister eyes boring down on him. He dared not look up. Answers would have to wait for another time. Time--was this a luxury that was slipping out of his control?

FBI HEADQUARTERS

"He never showed, Chief," said the man dejectedly as an older man entered the office. "Maybe he suspected they were following him."

"I hope that's the only reason, because if we lose him we're back to square one," said the younger man.

"I'd rather have him overly cautious and alive. We've waited this long. If we have to wait a little longer, so be it." Chief "Red" Saunders was speaking from a lifetime of experience that had taught him the gift of patience. He thoughtfully squinted at nothing on his desk and ran a strong hand through hair that had earned him his nickname - less red now that it had silver to tone it down. This case alone had probably contributed more character lines to his face and gray to his hair than any other.

Ben Griffin had been assigned to work on the case with Saunders. They were a good team. Ben was a little headstrong, but the Chief's years of experience helped keep things in perspective.

"I know, Chief; I'm just anxious to talk to him. He needs to know the score and exactly how much danger he is in. I hope we don't scare him off when he learns the whole story, but we'll just have to take that chance. I really believe if we'd been more up front initially with Pete, he'd be alive today. And who knows, maybe we'd have a cap over this whole mess."

"We can't blame ourselves, Ben. Pete knew what was at stake. In this game one mistake is all you usually get. Unfortunately, Pete was the victim this time, but we can't quit.

"It took so long to get someone on the inside," continued the Chief. "It's entirely possibly we may never have an opportunity like this again. We'll just have to let this latest scenario play itself out and hope for the best."

"Pete gave us a lot to go on," said the younger agent called Ben. "If we can pass this on to Amico, we might nail those sons of bitches once and for all."

"Assuming he'll cooperate," cautioned the Chief. He'd been close to real progress too many times to hang all his hopes on one long shot.

The two officers had been working together in the ongoing investigation of the Scarletto Family for the past year. It was a stroke of luck when a friend of Pete Boggio, who happened to be in law enforcement, contacted the Bureau. Pete had accidentally discovered some unusual activities at Good Shepherd and had mentioned his suspicions to him.

It seemed Pete had awakened in the middle of the night. Unable to get back to sleep, he had gotten up to get a glass of milk. Passing the window, he had noticed some movement in the parking lot. This, in itself, was not unusual since death calls were made at all hours. What had caught his attention was that one man appeared to be struggling, and none of the three were familiar to him. Although the light was dim, he had seen that the man in the middle was bound and gagged. To his shock, they had entered the crematorium.

Pete had continued his vigil. A short time later only two men had reappeared. It had terrified him to imagine what may have happened, but he had to be sure.

After waiting a reasonable time, which to Pete had seemed like an eternity, he had carefully made his way through the shadows to the rear of the crematorium. If they had done what he feared, there would be noise coming from the oven, and the walls would be warm. He had pressed his ear to the wall and immediately recoiled in horror. There was no question about it - something or someone was being incinerated.

Pete had related this incident to his friend who immediately contacted the local bureau chief, Red Saunders. He knew Red had been investigating the Scarletto Family off and on for several years and would welcome any lead. Red was a veteran FBI agent and had been aware of the alleged underworld activities of the Scarletto Family for almost 30 years. Like everyone else, he had endured the frustration of never being able to obtain enough evidence to prosecute.

When he had received the news of Pete's discovery, he was elated. Red had immediately contacted Ben Griffin whom he thought to be one of the brightest young stars of the Bureau. Ben, only thirty-five, had achieved a great deal of notoriety for his investigative prowess. They had made contact with Pete Boggio through his friend and convinced him to aid them in the investigation. They needed good solid evidence, and Pete might just be the break they'd been hoping for.

Things had progressed well but not to the point where arrests could be considered. They were fairly certain what had happened to the missing witnesses, but proving it was another thing. The last time they had contacted Pete he had said he was about to obtain evidence that would blow the case sky high. He had also mentioned that he thought he needed help. He had felt certain that it would come from a new apprentice by the name of Tony Amico. That was the last they had ever heard from him.

The so-called dead end was not yet exactly dead. If they could contact this fellow, Amico, without drawing attention to him, there was a chance he might cooperate. Knowing there was a real possibility of putting an innocent bystander in serious jeopardy, they had to be extremely cautious. They had finally succeeded through a lucky coincidence. One of their agents who worked strictly in the office presented the opportunity. His great uncle had passed away, and there was a slim chance contact could be made during the course of the funeral. It was their good fortune that Tony had been assigned to drive the family limousine, and contact had been made without incident.

When Tony had shown up at Nighttown, their spirits received a much-needed boost. His failure to appear at the designated rendezvous dashed their hopes just as quickly. They were, however, used to many setbacks and disappointments over the years. Hopefully, their perseverance would allow them another opportunity before Tony experienced the same fate as Pete.

21

Tony woke before his alarm went off, but he continued to lay in bed thinking. He had made up his mind that he was jumping into this thing with both feet no matter what the consequences. The most pressing matter was finding a way to get in touch with his contact without being followed. He had to assume that his every move was being closely observed. There had to be a way. He still felt he had the advantage since they could not be certain he was aware of their interest in him.

He had an idea. If he could get John Libertini to go out with him, maybe they would relax enough for him to make the much-needed contact at Nighttown. He reasoned they would allow Libertini to be his shadow and call the other goons off. It was worth a gamble. He somehow had to make a casual suggestion to a person with whom he had very little desire for social contact - someone he didn't like or trust. It couldn't appear contrived or he'd blow the whole thing.

The very next day fortune smiled on him and he had his opening. Tony and John were told to make a house call. They were to pick up a body in Wickliffe that afternoon.

John seemed unusually distant when they met at the garage. It may have been his imagination so Tony tried to break the ice.

"John, why don't you drive since you know this area like the back of your hand," suggested Tony. "I'm still feeling my way around these neighborhoods."

"Fine with me," said John abruptly.

"This is going to be tougher than I thought; he's not

exactly in a talkative mood," thought Tony. The cold silence was beginning to make him very anxious. "Mind if I turn on the radio?" he probed. "Do you like any particular type of music?" Searching for an opening, Tony said, "850 AM plays the big band sound. I like music from that era."

"As a matter of fact, so do I," said Libertini, perking up a bit. "I go out dancing and drinking as often as possible."

Seizing the opportunity, Tony said, "I think I saw you one night at Nighttown with a sweet young thing on your arm."

"You might have; I go there every chance I get. Food's good and so is the music."

"With this job and being new to the area, my social life has been a big fat zero," said Tony. "I haven't had a date for so long I feel like I'm in seminary."

This brought a slight chuckle from Libertini.

"Maybe he was loosening up," thought Tony. "I probably shouldn't ask this, but do you think your friend might have a friend for a lonely goomba?"

Libertini thought for a moment. "I'll see what I can do; you sound pretty desperate."

"Thanks, I didn't know it showed."

They both laughed and Tony suppressed a satisfied smile for the remainder of the trip. He didn't mention it again. Even a Cro-Magnon like Libertini might get the hint he was pushing a little too much.

———❧———

Bonitto's phone rang.

"Uncle Carlo, it's John."

"Well, what is it? Make it fast; I'm very busy." The irritation in his voice was evident, even to John.

"I'm sorry to bother you, but I think there is something you should know." He related the discussion he'd had with Tony earlier. "What do you want me to do,

Uncle Carlo?"

Carlo pondered the question for a moment. "By all means, get him a date. We haven't learned much using other methods; maybe this will bear better results. Maybe a pretty face and a few drinks may pry secrets out of him we haven't been able to get yet."

"It can't do any harm, and I know just the right person for the job," said Libertini excitedly.

"Good, John. They don't need to know anything about our motives. Just keep the conversation going and keep your ears open."

"I'm not certain he's even capable of doing two things at once," Bonitto mumbled to himself. "Find out what you can and give me a full report as soon as possible."

John was feeling quite full of himself, mistaking Bonitto's reaction for a show of confidence. "You can count on me, Uncle Carlo. I'll get some answers from that S.O.B."

"I'm sure you'll do your best, John. Now I must go." He hung up and sat there shaking his head. "I can't understand how my sister could have produced such an idiot. Louie had to have watered down the brains."

That evening about 7:30 Tony's phone rang. Half-dozing in front of the TV, he nearly jumped out of his chair. The voice at the other end was John's.

"The best I could do was a broad studying to be a nun, but I don't think you'll be disappointed. Who knows, after a night with you, she might want to renounce her vows," he joked.

"You're kidding," laughed Tony. "Do I detect a sense of humor? Someone else has to be writing his material. Putting two sentences together is a major accomplishment for this wing-nut," he thought.

"Yes, I'm kidding," said John. "You were the one who said you felt like you were in the seminary. But I do have a date for you. We'll pick them up at 7:30 Saturday evening and go to Nighttown for an evening of dinner, music and who knows what else."

"Sounds good to me. I hope I know how to act around someone of the opposite sex." Tony now had his chance. He only hoped the evening would provide an opportunity for contact. He prayed Carley would not be there too. Carley. He missed her. Though their encounters had been all too brief, she had made him feel like he'd never felt before.

At 7:30 sharp John pulled in front of the apartment and lightly honked the horn, jarring him out of blissful daydreaming.

"Real class," thought Tony. "At least he didn't yell out the window."

As he approached the car, John reached over and opened the front door on the passenger side. John was decked out in all his "Saturday Night Fever" splendor.

"He really outdid himself tonight. Just when I thought he couldn't get more outrageous!" thought Tony.

"Hop in," directed John. "We're going to meet them at Nighttown later. Your date had to work overtime so Gina's brother will drop them off. We can have a few drinks before they arrive. It'll loosen you up a bit."

"Good idea; maybe she won't be able to tell I haven't had contact with a living female under seventy-five in the last four months."

Libertini laughed. "We're already checked out with the housemother at the gate. We have to be back by midnight or this car turns into a pumpkin."

"This guy actually has some sense of humor," thought Tony. "Maybe he's not quite as big a dork as I thought. It could be a mistake to underestimate him."

They sat at the bar and exchanged small talk for about twenty minutes. Fortunately, there was no sign of Carley. As much as he missed her, he was relieved.

"Wait till you get a load of Gina. She's a real foxy broad. Not too bright, but who needs a broad with brains? When we go dancing, every eye in the joint is on us. A lot of guys would like to get their hands on her ass, but they know better."

"You two engaged or something?"

"I don't tie myself down to one broad," he bragged. "She knows better than to mess around with other dudes, and they keep their distance if they know what's good for them."

"He's already getting on my nerves," thought Tony. "I hope I can hang on until the girls get here."

Since the girls had not yet arrived, they ordered another round of drinks. Tony hoped there had been enough time for the contact to be made. Maybe the presence of Libertini would scare them off. He'd wait a little longer and then excuse himself and head for the restroom.

Just as he was about to make his move, Libertini exclaimed, "Here come the broads, late as usual. I feel like I spend half my life waiting on this bimbo."

As the girls entered the bar, Tony rose to meet them. True to form, John remained seated.

"It's about time, Gina," said Libertini as he finally rose to give her a casual peck on the cheek. "Gina and Diane, meet Tony Amico. He hasn't had a date in four months so watch out!"

Tony blushed and extended his hand in greeting. "It's been at least that long, but it appears the wait was worth it."

Now it was Diane's turn to blush, accompanied by an embarrassed giggle. They were both attractive, albeit with an overabundance of eye shadow and makeup. They were a little overdressed for Tony's tastes, but they fit perfectly with most of the clientele at Nighttown. Once they began talking and he was able to get a closer look, Tony guessed they were barely twenty years old. However, guessing a woman's age was definitely not his forte.

Diane was friendly enough, but he had to pry sentences out of her. She was constantly tugging at her dress or toying with her hair in between glances around the restaurant. Meaningful conversation did not appear to be one of her strengths.

"She's probably more nervous than me or, more likely, bored out of her gourd," thought Tony as they were seated at a table near the piano.

On the other hand, Gina's mouth never stopped. She was very skilled at talking and cracking gum at the same time.

"This could get old real fast," thought Tony. "They make a perfect couple."

About the time they ordered dinner, the band was making its appearance. Tony hardly noticed the individual members even though he was facing them. Once they began to play, he realized something that grabbed his attention. The piano player looked exactly like the same person who had handed him the $20 bill with the note attached. He'd only seen him once so he couldn't be absolutely certain. If it was, he had to act fast and attempt to make contact.

"Do any of you know the piano player?" he asked.

Gina spoke up. "I don't know his name, but he has filled in once or twice when we've been here. Only reason I remember is that he's a lot cuter than the regular guy," giggled Gina between snaps.

Neither John nor Diane responded other than to shake their heads. It was obvious Libertini did not appreciate Gina's remarks. It appeared John possessed a rather heavy streak of jealousy.

"This guy must really be insecure, getting uptight over such an innocent remark," thought Tony.

"I think I know the guy; he's from my hometown." Seizing the moment, Tony pressed on, saying, "You know how it is when you see someone out of context. I never expected to see someone I knew here." It sounded reasonable enough, and no one seemed too concerned with his explanation. "I'd like to go up and say 'hello' when they take a break," ventured Tony. "Maybe he'll come over to the table so Gina can meet him." The girls giggled, but John was not amused. The look on his face now hinted at more than just a trace of hostility.

They finished their meal about the time the band was concluding its set. Tony excused himself and walked over to the pianist. As he neared, their eyes met in recognition. Tony was smiling and extended his hand in greeting.

"You know me. We are both from Chagrin Falls. Act like we're old friends."

The man immediately grinned and started nodding. "381-1717 anytime night or day," he said through his smile.

"I said you'd come over to the table to meet everyone," explained Tony. "Just follow my lead. They don't know a thing about me so I can say anything and they'll swallow it." He said the phone number to himself several times as they headed back to the table.

"John, Gina and Diane, meet --." Tony's knees almost buckled as he'd forgotten to invent a name. The stranger quickly picked up on Tony's dilemma.

"I could tell you were going to introduce me as Fudge Baker. Nobody ever called me by my real name - I'll bet you don't even know it."

Regaining his composure, Tony countered, "You'd lose your bet, Frank, but I admit I had a momentary mental blackout. I could hardly believe my eyes. You really haven't changed much."

"I still live in Chagrin. I come here once in a while as a favor to a friend."

"Can you stay for a drink?" asked Tony. "Gina especially wanted to meet you; she thinks you're cute." Tony couldn't resist the opportunity. He was enjoying the snarl appearing on John's lips.

"Sorry, as much as I'd like to, I have to get back. Being a sub, we didn't get time to rehearse. Maybe I'll stop over later this evening. I seldom have the opportunity to meet such attractive ladies."

Libertini's jaw muscles tightened, but he showed restraint out of character for him.

With that Frank rose and gallantly kissed Gina on her hand as he left. She giggled uncontrollably. Immediately Libertini grabbed her arm and jumped to his feet.

"Get up, we're outta here," he snarled, pulling Gina to her feet. Apparently familiar with the extent of his temper and not wishing a confrontation, she rose without a word. He dragged her out of the restaurant. Diane meekly followed, totally embarrassed by Libertini's outburst. Tony trailed the three as they made a hasty exit.

"Mission accomplished. I never thought it would be so easy and so enjoyable," he mused, hardly able to suppress the grin.

As they were leaving the restaurant, the one thing Tony dreaded most happened. Carley was just coming in. Tony's jaw dropped and his eyes grew wide, but he couldn't acknowledge her. He prayed she would return the snub. He quickly regained his composure and painfully looked right through her as they actually brushed against one another. While passing her, he held his breath. To his relief, there was no reaction, and the door closed behind them. His heart was heavy. He hoped someday to be able to explain and that she would understand and be forgiving. For now, that would have to wait - too much was at stake.

Needless to say, on the ride back the atmosphere was quite cool, with the silence punctuated by an occasional crack of Gina's gum. John's reckless driving gave a clear indication of his foul mood. Diane whispered several apologies that Tony acknowledged with a shake of his head. He wished he could enjoy this scenario to its fullest, but Carley occupied his thoughts.

Libertini pulled up in front of what was apparently Gina's apartment and looked straight ahead. Taking the not-too-subtle hint, she opened the door and got out of the car. Before closing the door she said, "Nice to meet you, Tony. Diane, why don't you come in - it's still early."

Diane excused herself with a nervous peck on Tony's cheek and was out the door. Libertini peeled away, leaving about two inches of rubber and throwing Tony back against the seat.

"Easy," said Tony suppressing a snicker.

"That broad makes me crazy. You didn't help matters by inviting that dude over."

"I didn't realize your relationship was so insecure; otherwise I wouldn't have," said Tony, biting his lip.

"You haven't had a date in four months. You were better off and didn't realize it. Women - they're nothing but a big pain in the ass."

He pulled into the funeral home and stopped abruptly at Tony's apartment.

"Thanks, John, I appreciate you fixing me up. In spite of it all, I had a good time most of the evening."

"Whatever," muttered John as he pulled away.

"381-1717," said Tony as he climbed the stairs to his apartment. The success of the evening was diminished by the encounter with Carley. He fought the temptation to call her. Gritting his teeth, he grudgingly tried to erase the unfortunate incident from his mind. Sleep would be a scarce commodity again.

22

There was a meek tap on the office door.

"Come in," resounded with a tone that made John seriously consider if he should.

Even Carlo's invitations had an air of foreboding that always made one wonder if he really meant it or was actually saying, "Don't bother me, stay out of my sight."

John was definitely feeling the latter as he cautiously entered the room. He needed a good spin on his report in order to avoid Carlo's wrath. He was really sick and tired of being harassed by his uncle. Self-preservation was going to force him to lie through his teeth. He wasn't up to another ass chewing by dear old Uncle Carlo.

"Well, don't just stand in the doorway. Come in and let's have it," was about as warm a reception as Carlo could muster. He really wasn't optimistic about receiving any earth-shattering news. He gave John little credit for doing anything efficiently. If it weren't for his sainted sister, this toad would be mixing cement for one of the local masonry contractors or better yet, planted in it.

"Not much to report, Uncle Carlo," said John haltingly.

"Why am I not surprised? Did you notice anything at all out of the ordinary?" Carlo really didn't expect anything but enjoyed watching his nephew squirm. This pastime made being forced to employ the incompetent John almost worth the trouble.

"I really put him through a good grilling," lied John. "Things I figured were sure to trip him up. He's one smart cookie."

"How could you possibly detect that? I can't believe you came back without one single clue."

John slouched noticeably and then his face brightened. "There was one thing. He brought a guy from the band over to the table. They seemed to be old friends, but it looked a little fishy to me."

He was on a roll now. Maybe he could save face with this one if he really milked it. "This dude definitely looked suspicious to me." He now had piqued Carlo's interest.

"Go on," he said impatiently. "Why did you think so?"

"Just little sly looks and their body language." John was really getting carried away.

Carlo looked at him suspiciously. "Anything more concrete than sly looks and body language?"

"Not exactly, but I just felt there was more to it." He was starting to squirm again.

"That's great news. I'm going to run up to tell Mr. Scarletto that my brilliant nephew thinks Amico was contacted by a guy in the band through mental telepathy."

Libertini knew enough to keep his mouth shut and backed out of the room like he was exiting an audience with the Pope. Once out the door, he squared his shoulders and regained his usual arrogant posture.

"That's gratitude for you. I risk my neck to get information and he treats me like dirt. If he weren't Mama's brother, I'd personally whack him. Why did I ever agree to come here in the first place? This job is making me nuts. I'll tell Mama she's got to get me out of this friggin place."

Carlo sat at his desk, thoughtfully rubbing his temples. As much as he hated to admit it, possibly John had accidentally stumbled onto something.

The restaurant was a common, innocent enough meeting place. If a member of the band were, in fact, a possible contact, it would be quite easy to do. Too much was at stake. No bit of information would go without a follow-up. It was a reach, but it had to be pursued. He quickly rose and went to the window.

John was just storming down the back steps. Bonitto tapped on the glass loudly. John turned to see Carlo motioning him back up to the office.

"Oh, shit," hissed John as he grudgingly returned to his personal hell on earth.

Entering the office, he was shocked to see Carlo's demeanor had amazingly changed for the better.

"Sit down, John. I've been giving some thought to what you just told me."

Libertini was puzzled by this change in attitude. Carlo's tone was more amicable.

"There could possibly be something to what you observed."

John tilted his head and listened.

"We can't afford to leave anything to chance. What was Amico's friend's name?"

The brief elation he had previously experienced now returned to status quo. He couldn't tell Carlo he hadn't bothered to remember a name because he had been consumed with petty jealousy. Preparing for another berating, he hung his head and mumbled.

"You what?" sneered Carlo. "I try to show confidence in you by entrusting you with an important job - one that could possibly prevent the downfall of the Family - and what do you do? You don't even pay enough attention to remember a name. Only one name! You never cease to amaze me. I want you to go to Nighttown tonight and see if you can get that guy's name. If he is a contact, the name will probably be phony. That, in and of itself, will tell us all we need to know. Do you think you can handle that?"

"Yes, Uncle Carlo," he meekly replied. "You can count on me."

"Based on your track record, that is something that remains to be seen. Now go and try to do it without attracting unnecessary attention."

John was about to repeat the "You can count on me" line, but thought better of it. Why invite more abuse? He simply nodded and quickly left the office.

John grudgingly dialed Gina's number at work. He was going to have to eat more crow.

A familiar voice said, "Salerno Landscaping, how can we help you."

Speaking through clenched teeth he announced, "It's John. I'm sorry about last night. I shouldn't have gotten so mad about something stupid like you talking to some stranger. By the way, what was that dude's name?"

"Apology accepted. Why do you want to know his name? Are you going to put out a contract on him?"

"Don't be crazy, Gina, you know I'm not into that stuff. I was just curious."

"That's what ticks me off about you, John. You get upset and ruin a perfectly great evening. I don't even remember his name. That's how important it was. You had to make a big deal out of nothing and spoil everyone's fun."

Another chewing out in one day was more than he could take. He was fighting back the urge to take all his frustrations out on Gina. Miraculously, he resisted the impulse. In a forced voice oozing with sweetness and humility, he pleaded. "That's why I called. I realize I was way out of line, and I want to make it up to you. Let's go out tonight. Let me prove to you how sorry I am. We'll go to Nighttown and if that dude comes over, I'll treat him like a goomba."

Gina was speechless. This was so out of character. There had to be a hidden agenda. Maybe he was going to whack them both. She quickly dismissed that scenario with a shake of her head, and haltingly replied, "How many times do I have to swallow that line? You're beginning to sound like a broken record."

"I mean it, Gina," he lied. "Just give me one more chance." He almost said "please", but no one, not even Uncle Carlo, could make him use that word.

"O.K John, one more chance. I'll be ready by 7:30. If you embarrass me just once more with your childish behavior, I'll never speak to you again. You could come crawling back and I'll turn my back and walk away. Grow up!"

She hung up the phone, not knowing what to expect from her dim-witted boyfriend. She smiled, impressed at the way she had talked to him, not realizing his true motives.

John sat there, his face contorted, veins protruding from his head and neck. The nerve of that broad, talking to him like that. What he ought to do is slap her around until she learned some respect. If they could get something on Amico, it would be worth the humiliation he had endured. Paybacks for Uncle Carlo and Gina could be waiting down the road. Nobody could treat him that way without living to regret it. A sinister smile crept over his face as he fantasized the ways he would make them pay. For now the task at hand was exposing someone he hated even more: Tony Amico.

23

Tony still had a gigantic problem. He could not use the phone in his apartment, and it was obvious he was being followed. At least he knew how to make contact. All he had to do was figure out how to make the call undetected. The only phone he was certain about was the one in Pete's apartment, but making an attempt to go over there could be very risky. If he were seen, it would be all over. So Pete's apartment was out of the question. Again the realization jolted him that he was, in a true sense, their prisoner. Sure, he was free to move about, but the constraints were such that he was not truly free. He had to constantly be on the defensive, knowing his every move was under intense scrutiny.

He sat there blankly staring at the TV when suddenly a commercial appeared that gave him an idea. If he could get a cellular phone without anyone's knowledge, he could call undetected. Obtaining a phone presented another problem, but he felt that that hurdle could be overcome. Mulling the question for some time, he finally came up with a plan. He would place an order for the phone through the mail and have it delivered to a post office box. Even this had some risk involved. He was sure of being followed. Why was he going to the post office? To alleviate suspicion, he rigged up a dummy parcel and addressed it to Uncle Gino. Each trip to the post office could involve mailing a package.

The next day, after obtaining a post office box, he purchased a money order for the cost of the phone. The request for the phone, along with the money order, was mailed at the same time. Now all he could do was wait.

Hoping not to arouse suspicion, he allowed a week to

pass before making his next trip to the post office. Unfortunately, the box was empty. He anxiously waited two more days before his next attempt. Each time he entered the lobby, the same man had followed him in.

"This is not a coincidence," thought Tony as he cautiously observed his watchdog. Appearing nonchalant, he was able to get a good look at his adversary.

The man's most striking feature was his extremely thin body. It was difficult to estimate his age. Tony guessed he was younger than he appeared. His body was curled forward at the waist and his shoulders hunched up, almost obscuring his head. He looked as if he were in constant pain. His long pointed nose and beady eyes gave him a rodent-like appearance.

"It wouldn't be hard to pick him out in a line-up. He'd make a great character in a Dick Tracy Comic," thought Tony as he opened his post office box.

To his disappointment, there was only a letter. In it was his original money order with a note attached:

Dear Mr. Amico: Thank you for your interest in CelComm. Unfortunately, company policy prevents us from doing mail order business. All contracts must be consummated in person. We are sorry for any inconvenience it may have caused. If we can be of further service, please do not hesitate to contact us at 1-800-CEL-COMM.
*   --Sincerely, Jacob Stilson.*

"Now what?" thought Tony angrily. "Back to square one and I'm running out of options." As he left the post office, he noticed a black sedan with tinted windows parked just around the next corner. The man who had also been in the post office was just getting in it.

"Let's find out if I'm imagining this one." He crossed the street and entered a Convenient Food Mart. At the deli counter that faced the door, he ordered a half-pound of tuna salad. Presently the door opened and a man entered. Other than the fact he was wearing sunglasses on a cloudy day, he did not look out of the ordinary. Compared to his accomplice, he looked like someone your sister might bring home to meet the folks. He started circling the aisles, picking up a few items along the way. Tony watched him out of the corner of his eye as he paid for his purchase and hurried toward the exit.

Tony walked briskly to his car and got in. As he looked in the rear view mirror, he could see the man from the store running back toward the parked car. As Tony pulled out from the curb, his escort was already turning the corner.

Heading back to the funeral home, his mind was in a whirl. The preoccupation with his dilemma was so intense that he didn't even bother to note whether the black sedan was still in pursuit as he entered the grounds.

How long could this cat and mouse game continue? Frankly, he was a bit puzzled that they hadn't made their move by now. Obviously his activities had been suspicious, especially since they already had considered him potentially dangerous enough to warrant all this attention. What were they waiting for? Why was he still free to move about? It couldn't go on much longer. He prayed all their attention was on him and not Carley. It was driving him crazy not being able to talk to her, but he refused to weaken. Not until it was all over one way or another. He was convinced he had to act fast. The sick feeling in the pit of his stomach seemed to tell him it was tonight or never.

——————

"How much longer are we going to play games with this dude?" asked Squeeky. "We've already given him more slack than he deserves. If it were up to me, he'd be history by now."

"You'll continue to do as you're told for as long as it takes." It was the voice of an irritated Carlo Bonitto. "I hope we never reach the point where any decision making is left to you two. You have a job to do; hopefully it can be done with some degree of efficiency in spite of your limited abilities. Unless you have something important to report, don't call us, we'll call you."

With that he hung up the phone. The frustration on his face indicated he shared some of the concerns voiced by Squeeky. However, he would never reveal his distress to subordinates. They looked to him for leadership and held him in a kind of fearful admiration. Any perceived crack in his armor would be interpreted as a sign of weakness. He knew if this ever happened, his usefulness to the Family would be over and he would become expendable. They could not afford to have someone in his position that was not in total control of any situation. This harsh reality was accepted because it was dependent on survival. His loyalty would not permit him to question any decisions coming from the Hill.

Still, he was becoming increasingly unnerved by the whole situation. Couldn't his loyalty be used as an excuse to reconfirm his suspicions to them and hope for their reconsideration? He knew not to step over the line for he was well aware of his place in the hierarchy. Desperate times called for desperate measures. Maybe he could subtly nudge them into action. It was nothing personal. Tony was actually more the kind of person he had vainly hoped his nephew could have become. But now he posed a major threat, and the time to act had come. He only hoped it was not too late.

Carlo quickly dialed the number and anxiously waited for an answer. After four rings a message informed him no one was available to answer and would he please leave a message.

"It's Carlo," he announced and hung up. Immediately the phone rang, and Carlo hurriedly returned the phone to his ear.

"How can we help you, Carlo?"

"Mr. Scarletto," he began, "I realize the circumstances are quite different with this one, but there is so much at stake. I fully understand your family loyalty in this case, but Amico knows nothing of this. He knows nothing of our world."

"You have every right to be concerned, my friend," returned Scarletto. "Reluctantly, I am forced to agree with you. However, my father is not as easily persuaded. Being of the old ways, he feels the debt is yet to be paid. I'm afraid age has somewhat replaced rational thinking. He's blinded to the danger this man can bring to our house."

"Mr. Scarletto, we still have all the evidence that can connect him to the murder scene in Toledo. There are eyewitnesses from the restaurant and the woman's home. All we have to do is make a phone call and provide an anonymous tip to the police where the murder weapon is. His fingerprints are all over it. It would be a handy bargaining chip in exchange for his silence."

"Think about it, Carlo," he interrupted. "We then put ourselves in a very compromising position. Suppose he agrees to keep quiet. Now he not only knows for certain we have removed Pete Boggio, but that we are also responsible for the death of that unfortunate woman. What assurance do we have that he will remain cooperative? Mr. Amico then holds the bargaining chip, my friend. Do you doubt for one second that the authorities would not gladly trade one insignificant murder suspect for the chance to bring our entire house down?"

Carlo immediately realized that his tactical blunder could undermine their confidence in him. "I beg your pardon, Mr. Scarletto," said an embarrassed Bonitto. "It was stupid of me to even think such a thing would be possible."

"Don't be so hard on yourself, my friend. Your loyalty momentarily replaced reason. For this we cannot fault you. We were able to find the woman and take care of that problem so no harm has been done. I'm afraid when we reach the point of having to resort to any kind of deal Amico will have to be eliminated. I can assure you we are discussing the possibility at this very moment."

"I fully understand and appreciate your attitude," interrupted Bonitto respectfully. "I would not call your attention to this matter if I were not very concerned. Hopefully, any damage to the Family is minimal at this point in time, but I fear that could change even as we speak."

"Believe me, Carlo, we respect your opinion. Your concerns will be relayed to my father immediately."

"I can only hope they will realize the folly of prolonging the inevitable."

"Meanwhile, keep a close watch over him, and if there is anything out of the ordinary, you know what you must do. Your men can follow the usual procedure."

"We're poised waiting for your word," responded Bonitto confidently.

"Good, my loyal friend. You will hear from us soon." With that, Vito Scarletto hung up.

Carlo sat nervously twisting his diamond ring and gazing out the window. Presently he rose and walked over to a large cabinet. Withdrawing a key, he opened the oaken doors. His hand wrapped around a small pearl-handed pistol that he placed in his coat pocket. He returned to his desk and nervously waited for the call he knew would soon come.

By the time Tony reached his apartment he had decided upon his course of action. He couldn't afford the luxury of more time. Caution was no longer an option. His survival depended on making the first move. He would attempt another bicycle ride to the phone booth in the Metropark. He fervently hoped they would not be making their move sooner. He shivered as he pondered the distinct possibility of not living to see another day. He truly felt this cloak-and-dagger business had finally reached a climax.

At 11:30 he removed the bicycle from the rack and silently walked it out toward the gate. In spite of the cool night air, perspiration soaked his clothing in a matter of minutes. The darkness provided adequate cover as long as he moved quietly. He was progressing nicely until he turned the corner of the hedge near the gate. He stopped abruptly.

At the entrance to the parkway was the now-familiar black sedan. Fortunately, the moon was behind a heavy bank of clouds. How long he would have the advantage of increased darkness was questionable. But it was a chance he had to take. He slid silently into the shadows along the line of hedges and quietly paused. How much more could his nerves take? Fortunately, the car was parked on the other side of the road facing the entrance of Good Shepherd.

His mind went over the incidents leading up to this point. For someone who had led a rather boring existence, this was so wild he couldn't believe it. Why was he risking his life? He could have walked away at the first sign of anything out of the ordinary. Why didn't he have the good sense to get out of this mess before it was too late? His strong sense of right and wrong had pushed him to this point, and in spite of everything, he knew this is what he had to do. The reality of it all made him shudder. If he survived this, which seemed very unlikely, the biggest risk he would take for the rest of his days would be purchasing a lottery ticket.

Tony waited, hardly able to breathe. A car was approaching. It would provide additional cover. He quickly slipped around the hedges and into the shadowed haven the Metroparks provided.

He waited for several minutes before he felt it was safe to begin riding. He pedaled furiously as if he was being pursued by the devil himself. He didn't know how long it took to reach his destination. He finally arrived at the phone booth, dropped the bike and rushed over to dial the number. A sharp click indicated the phone at the other end was picked up but there was no response.

Tony feverishly waited a few seconds and then spoke. "Hello, is anyone there? This is Tony Amico. I was given this number..."

"Yes, Tony," a voice interrupted. "We're glad to hear from you. We were beginning to fear the worst. My name is Ben Griffin. FBI. I'm the one who sent you the note. Pete Boggio told us we might be able to count on you."

"I think I have a rough idea of what's going on, but you'll have to fill me in regarding the big picture," panted Tony. "Do you have anything on Pete?"

"Yes. We believe Pete was murdered by your employers, and if the MO is consistent with other victims, he was incinerated in their crematorium."

Tony's worst nightmare was coming true. He had actually expected this response, but it didn't prevent him from uttering a gasp and swallowing hard to keep from gagging. He slumped against the wall of the phone booth, staring as if in a trance as the agent continued.

"The Scarletto Family has a long history. We believe

they are responsible for most every type of major underworld activity in the Cleveland area for the past sixty plus years. You'd think we could have come up with enough evidence for a conviction by now. Believe me; better men than I have tried with no success. The problem is linked to the disappearance of potential witnesses. We are aware of at least a dozen cases, and there may be more. Other suspects go to jail without saying a single word. Their loyalty has been unflinching.

Pete was the first break we've had in well over a year. He mentioned a book or log that he felt contained some sort of record of these executions. He had accidentally come across it one day while working in the crematorium. Their reaction told him it was something not meant for his eyes. He never saw it again until a week before he disappeared.

"For several months he kept us informed of all legitimate cremations. We compared this to East Ohio Gas Company's records of usage. There was an excessive amount of gas used when no cremations were scheduled. There was no doubt in his mind that the crematorium was used for this purpose. Tony, if such a log exists and you could get it, we would be eternally grateful. Obviously, there are tremendous risks involved. I think you are already well aware of that fact. This book would provide us with enough evidence to indict these scumbags even without victims to back us up. We could identify the crematorium as the murder weapon."

Tony felt like he was trapped in the middle of a bad dream. He was hearing words being spoken, but it seemed so unreal. As they echoed around in his head, he wanted to awaken and have it all disappear. He wished he were back home in Chagrin Falls working for Don, but the uncompromising truth was that it was too late; he was in far over his head. There was no escaping the fact that his life could end abruptly. He shook his head just in time to hear a question that made him shudder.

"Can we count on you, Tony? We'll do everything in our power to protect you and your family."

"Just like you protected Pete? I'm sorry, that wasn't fair," he said before the agent could respond. "I'm into something I never bargained for, but I'm positive they are about to make their move soon. What's kept them at bay up to this point is just a stay of execution as far as I can tell. They could be plotting my demise at this very moment." Tony couldn't believe he was actually verbalizing the fears that had been careening around in his brain for weeks. In spite of the threatening predicament, there was a bizarre sense of relief in finally being able to express his alarm to someone.

"At this stage of the game, I don't really have a choice," said Tony.

"Probably not, to be brutally honest with you. Unfortunately you're right; they could possibly be planning another barbecue right now."

"That's exactly how I feel, too; so let's go for it!" He couldn't believe these words were coming from him.

"That's what we had hoped you'd say," replied Griffin. "If we are successful, we will be in your debt."

"It's the *if* that disturbs me," returned Tony, his voice trembling.

"You have every right to feel concern," said Ben. "No way can we minimize the risk involved."

"My problem won't be getting back undetected, but where I go from there is a huge question mark," replied Tony. "I'm on a really short tether, and I fear it's getting shorter all the time. Somehow I've got to get into the crematorium undetected. If I draw a crowd, I'm toast - probably literally!"

"I didn't want to have to bring this up," said Ben, "but you may have to use the gun we left with you."

"I know," gulped Tony, "that's an option I've been dreading."

"One more thing," said Ben. "If you'll look down in the slot where the phone book is usually located, you'll find a small cell phone wrapped in plastic. Our number is already activated so all you have to do is push the call button."

Tony removed the phone and placed it in his pocket.

"Tony, if in your judgment the situation is becoming too perilous," cautioned Ben, "don't hesitate to call us. I guarantee we'll be swarming around the place in minutes. One more innocent life lost is not worth the risk. As added insurance, keep the cell phone with you at all times. And don't forget the gun!"

That's comforting," said Tony. "I'll be in touch; maybe we'll get lucky. One more thing. Can you do me a favor, Ben?"

"You name it, and I'll do my best."

"There's a girl who tends bar at Nighttown. Her name is Carley Benton, and her life could be in danger. I hope it's not already too late. Could you have someone pick her up and put her in protective custody?"

"Sure thing, Tony. I'll send an agent over right away. We'll have her safe and sound in less than ten minutes."

"Thanks a million, Ben," said a much-relieved Tony.

"No problem. Be careful, Tony," said Ben, understating the obvious.

He hung up the phone, realizing he had just dug a hole from which he probably would not escape. "No one lives forever," he said with little conviction in his voice, "but I had foolishly hoped to get in a few more years before becoming a vital statistic." He slumped against the wall of the phone booth, lowered his head and began praying. Tony's prayers had always been for others, but tonight had to be an exception.

⸺➤•◦•◀⸺

When Bonitto's phone rang, he knew who would be at the other end of the line.

"Carlo, my father has finally given his approval. Do what you have to do. This problem must be eliminated as soon as possible."

"Good - you must have been very persuasive. I realize it was difficult for him to give the order."

"Not so, Carlo. When it clearly becomes a question of the Family's survival, the decision is simplified. Do it quickly and clean." He hung up.

Bonitto picked up the phone and dialed John Libertini's number. He had to admit that under other circumstances Tony Amico was not someone he would relish exterminating. He grudgingly admitted a slight admiration for his next victim. His biggest concern now was leaving such an important task to an incompetent fool like his nephew. He shuddered at the thought.

"John, this is Uncle Carlo. I have a job for you. Go to Amico's apartment under the pretext of going on a death call. Get him out to the Metropark and my two boys will take over."

"It's about time," agreed John. "I never trusted that S.O.B. from the beginning. It'll be a death call all right, and it'll be a pleasure."

"You're wasting time. Start using your brain instead of your mouth and get moving."

"Yes, Uncle Carlo, whatever you say." He mumbled some unintelligible comment that it was fortunate for him Carlo did not hear.

Libertini went to Tony's apartment with a smug look of satisfaction. He couldn't wait to confront his nemesis. He knocked on the door loudly several times without a response. After repeated knocking and calling, he forced the door open and found the apartment empty. He quickly dialed Bonito's number.

"He's not here, Uncle Carlo, maybe he's onto us."

"Brilliant deduction, genius. It's 1:00 a.m. and he's not in his apartment. What could possibly be unusual about that? Is his car in the garage?"

"I'll check," said Libertini. He rushed out of the apartment, down the steps and raised the garage door.

Shortly he returned and breathlessly announced, "The car is there, but I know there was a bicycle in the garage. It's gone!"

"He can't be far," said Carlo, now becoming excited instead of irritated. "Get the boys and go in opposite directions. I want Tony back here before daylight. Do it anyway you have to, but get him here. I'll be at the crematorium."

Libertini went out and told Carlo's henchmen of Tony's disappearance. The sedan headed south and Libertini headed north through the Metropark. He carefully searched the shadows but with no success. Disappointed, he approached the end of the parkway. He saw activity at the phone booth, and a satisfied smile crossed his face. There, just getting on his bicycle, was his prey. Tony looked up just in time to see Libertini's car come to a screeching stop. Before he could react, John was out of the car pointing a snub-nosed pistol at him.

"Late night workout? I didn't realize you were such a fitness nut," smirked Libertini as he aimed the menacing-looking weapon at his head. "Get in the car and you drive," he commanded.

"What's this all about, John?" asked Tony in a vain attempt at naivete.

"Don't give me that innocent bull shit. I think you know what this is all about. Now shut your face and get in the car, smart-ass. You'll find out soon enough."

He got in as Libertini entered the passenger side. The pistol was just a few inches from his head.

"Back to the funeral home fast; we have a warm reception waiting. How do you want it - medium or well done?" laughed Libertini. "If it was up to me, I'd waste you right here. It'd give me more satisfaction watching you die."

Tony could hardly control his shaking body as he stumbled into the car. "I guess this means they're onto me," he said in a quivering voice.

"That's right, genius," John said mockingly. "You've answered the $64,000 question. Let's go get your reward!"

Fortunately, the terror he felt had not completely blocked out his will to survive. He noticed John, as usual, had not bothered to fasten his seat belt. Even in his highly excitable state, this was automatic with Tony. Driving along the parkway, Tony decided to take a gamble that could cost him his life sooner than Libertini was anticipating. He took a deep breath and mumbled a prayer.

Rounding a corner, he slammed the gas pedal to the floor and continued to turn the wheel sharply. He shot across the road heading directly for a large oak tree at the very edge of the curve. Tony closed his eyes tightly and gripped the steering wheel with all his strength. The head-on crash hurled him forward, but the explosive force of the air bag stopped him.

Everything went blank in the suffocating silence that surrounded him. It was over in the blink of an eye. His passenger was not quite so fortunate. With no air bag for protection and no time to react, a horrified John Libertini was catapulted face first through the windshield. He sprawled motionless across the hood as blood slowly seeped from what had been his face an instant earlier.

Though it seemed much longer, Tony regained his senses within a few seconds. He laboriously climbed out of the car and staggered over to Libertini's lifeless body. He recoiled at the sight. Tony's life-threatening gamble had paid off. The hunter had become the prey.

After retrieving Libertini's gun and placing it in his pocket, he tried to start the car but with no success. Steam hissed from the cracked radiator. On the second try the motor sluggishly turned over. It creaked and groaned, slowly dislodging itself from the sturdy oak. Miraculously, he was able to maneuver the car a short distance, partially concealing it in the underbrush.

Though he was almost delirious, there was no time to waste. He began the painful jog back to the funeral home. By this time adrenaline had taken total control of his body. It was a good thing he didn't have far to go. He had no idea what had transpired causing John to be sent looking for him. One thing was certain - they would be expecting him one way or another very soon.

His fragmented plan was to drive back and load Libertini's body into a hearse and return to the crematorium. What might happen after that was anybody's guess. If they were planning another execution, it's very possible the log Ben had mentioned would be there. He would just have to play it by ear. There was no time to plot strategy more than one step at a time.

Except for a light in Bonitto's office, the building was dark as he slipped back into the grounds and quietly entered one of the garages. The keys were always left in the ignition as normal policy. He roared out of the lot and shot past the startled guard. Alerted to what was to go down tonight, Joseph recognized Tony's panic-stricken face. He immediately phoned Carlo with the news. But he was too late. Bonitto had already crossed the parking lot and was firing up the oven.

Joseph was confused. He was so used to taking orders that he had never made a decision on his own before. He nervously continued dialing Bonitto's number, letting it ring several times, hanging up, and repeating the whole procedure. His thoughtless lack of initiative bought precious minutes for Tony.

Just as Tony was approaching the entrance, the black sedan passed in front of him heading in the same direction. If they discovered Libertini's car, it would complicate matters far beyond his repair. He made up his mind to follow them at a safe distance with the headlights out and see what would happen next.

To his relief, the car passed without discovering the spot where the accident had occurred. It was critical that he acted fast because they would probably return this way soon. His body was racked with pain, but he could not let that interfere with what he had to do. The urgency of the moment allowed him to summon strength he never knew existed. His mind and body were operating in a zone that propelled him to a level beyond anything he had ever experienced.

Despite this, he had to swallow back his nausea as he laboriously removed the gurney and dragged John's bloody corpse into position. Buckling him in, he zipped up the body bag and slid the gurney into the hearse. It was none too soon, for as he pulled onto the Parkway, headlights showed in the rear view mirror. It had to be the black sedan, but there was no choice - back to the funeral home was the only option. He removed the cell phone from his pocket and punched the call button. To his relief, it was answered immediately.

"Ben?"

"Yes, Tony?"

"They're onto me. I'm going back to Good Shepherd with Libertini's body in the back of the hearse."

"What happened?"

"I don't have time to explain. I'll be pulling into Good Shepherd in a few minutes. I expect there'll be a reception figuring it's me in the back instead of Libertini. There's a car following me - a black sedan. Can you get through to someone to head them off? I'll slow down to give you more time."

"We'll do our best. If they're still on your tail when you get to the entrance, just drive on past until you see us. Then we'll stop them."

"O.K.", said Tony.

"What are you going to do if you get in?" asked Ben.

"I'm not sure yet, but I've got a crazy plan boiling in my head. Wish me luck!"

"Don't stick your neck out any further than necessary. We want you all in one piece. We'll be there as soon as we can."

Tony was beyond the greatest fright he'd ever experienced in his life. But strangely enough, there was no panic. He was cool and calculated. He did allow himself the futile wish that the sedan would follow him so he could drive past and forget the whole damn thing.

A police car came toward him with its lights flashing. He pulled over and watched through the mirror. The police car blocked the path of the sedan and Tony's fate was sealed. With his heart pounding, he pulled into Good Shepherd's grounds. The next few minutes would be the most critical of his life.

Suddenly Joseph appeared in his path. His eyes were wild, and he was waving a pistol menacingly. Shaking violently, he held up his free hand motioning him to stop.

Tony's instincts took over. He tapped the brake lightly to give the impression he was attempting to stop. The guard relaxed for just an instant. This gave Tony an opening, and immediately he took advantage. He punched the gas pedal to the floor and turned the wheel sharply. There was a loud thud as Joseph's body was sent flying over the hood, landing behind in a mangled heap. The sickening realization that he had possibly taken another human life caused him to gag. But he couldn't afford to dwell on Joseph's demise for more than an instant. His survival instincts forced him to refocus. He righted the car, turned off the headlights and headed for the crematorium and his confrontation with Carlo. There were no signs of life in the eerie silence of the darkened parking lot. Looming ahead at the rear of the lot stood the dreaded building, more foreboding than he could possibly imagine.

"I don't know whether silence is a good or bad sign," he sighed.

After backing in, he quickly got out and removed the gurney. He pushed it to the door, rang the bell and stepped back into the shadows. The hair was standing up on the back of his neck and he was breathing so fast he feared he'd hyperventilate. His eyes blurred as perspiration flooded them. He quickly wiped them just in time as the door slowly opened.

Outlined by the shaft of light was the menacing figure of Carlo. The puzzled look on his face only lasted a moment as Tony stepped out of the shadows with his gun drawn and pointed at his face.

"Step back in, Carlo, and pull the gurney with you. I think you'll be interested in its contents."

The oven was roaring. The heat it generated was almost suffocating.

Acting on instinct, Tony amazed himself with the cool efficiency in which he operated. Possibly Bonitto was too taken back to detect the slight quiver in his voice.

"What's the meaning of this?" demanded Bonitto. "Do you realize what you're doing? Put that gun down. No matter what happens to me, you'll never leave these grounds alive." His hand started slowly moving toward his coat pocket, hoping his intimidating voice and icy stare would provide a distraction.

"Maybe not," countered Tony, "but I won't be the only one going out feet first. For now, since I have the gun, just do as I say. If you move your hand one more inch, I'll blow you away on the spot."

Carlo started toward him but immediately thought better of it. He was keenly aware of the excited state his adversary was displaying. He retreated as Tony aimed the quivering gun at his head while grasping the handle of a nearby gurney and rolling it toward him.

"Unzip the bag and get in. Lay face down."

Gritting his teeth, Bonitto grudgingly obliged. Tony removed the pistol from his pocket and pulled the body straps up tightly, securing him. He then jerked Bonitto's head back, and stuffed a rubber glove in his mouth. He zipped up the bag to the sound of muffled protestations and prepared to push the squirming contents out to the hearse.

As he quickly glanced around the room, he saw an object that riveted his attention. On the desk was a small journal. It was opened to a page, blank except for one insert: "A.A. 9/15/98." It was meant to be the obituary of Anthony Amico. This had to be the log Pete had mentioned. How could they be so stupid to leave evidence of their crimes? Sure enough, on the previous page were the initials "P.B." Tony blinked away tears of rage as the reality of Pete's fate was staring up at him. It was obvious that he had joined the ranks of those who had had the misfortune of crossing the Scarletto Family. Obviously, this log surfaced from a very secure place only when a cremation was to occur.

"What incredible luck," thought Tony. He quickly leafed through the pages, and what he saw made him gasp. There were at least twenty entries containing the initials of those unfortunates who had threatened the Scarletto crime empire. He froze as he heard a voice coming from the open door.

"You've been a busy boy tonight, Tony. Don't turn around until you drop the gun and the book. That is, unless you want your body parts scattered all over this room."

Disbelieving his bad luck, Tony dropped the gun and turned to face Josh Benitt. Tony's heart sank. It looked like the unwanted adventure was finally going to come to an unfortunate conclusion. He pointed a shotgun that resembled a small cannon directly at Tony's midsection.

"You've been trouble from day one. Your final reward has been too long in coming. Where's Carlo?" he demanded.

Seizing the opportunity, Tony pushed the gurney toward Josh with his leg. "Unzip the body bag and see for yourself."

With a trembling hand, Josh began to unzip the bag, exposing the blood-soaked body of John Libertini. The gory sight distracted him just long enough to give Tony the advantage he had been waiting for.

He kicked the cart violently into Benitt's midsection, knocking him to the floor. The gurney toppled over, stunning him momentarily, and pinning him where he fell. Instantly, Tony was out the door and in the hearse before Josh could recover. The tires squealed as he raced across the parking lot heading for the gate. Benitt followed on foot waving the shotgun. He sprinted across the lot, angling behind the buildings in an effort to cut him off. Because he could crisscross the lawn, there was a chance he might reach the gate, foiling Tony's escape.

Tony was totally out of control. The hearse was bouncing off trees and through shrub beds. Waves of sparks shot out from the rocker panels as he scraped the tall curbs. He was barely able to negotiate the sharp curve that led to the gate, but a short straight-a-way allowed him precious seconds to right the vehicle. As he focused on the road ahead, he saw Josh aiming a sawed-off shotgun directly at him blocking the path.

As a cloud of smoke belched out, he ducked, and the hearse once more lurched out of control. The first blast had struck the right front tire. The hearse bounced off the high curb and veered sharply to the left. Josh was aiming the shotgun right at Tony's face and was no more than ten yards away.

Tony ducked below the steering wheel and pulled it sharply. He heard the shotgun blast and felt shards of glass fall on him. At about the same moment the hearse crashed explosively into the Gate House. Josh's agonizing scream was muted by the sound of the hearse tearing through the small building. It passed completely through the structure and reared up over the opposite curb. A small tree directly in its path snapped like a matchstick but did manage to finally bring the steaming vehicle to a halt. The abrupt stop threw Tony violently against the lower portion of the dashboard, and everything went blank.

25

THE COURTROOM

Carlo Bonitto and his two henchmen sat in total silence throughout the trial. Carlo never once looked in Tony's direction - never giving the slightest hint of recognition. From the time of their arrest to sentencing, they never changed expressions or uttered a single word to the authorities. The logbook had mysteriously disappeared. There was no evidence of a connection with the Scarlettos. The Family avoided any direct implication throughout the entire proceeding. Each mention of the Scarlettos was quickly met with an objection by the defense.

The judge grudgingly was forced to overrule each attempt by the prosecution to get the Scarlettos involved in the proceedings. Frustrations continued to mount as the trial neared its conclusion. Initially Ben Griffin and Chief Saunders had been optimistic, but as the trial progressed, they became painfully aware the results would be the same.

It was hoped that at least one of the accused would incriminate the Scarlettos, but their loyalty was unflinching. Carlo's icy composure never betrayed what might have been boiling inside. Even the two "banana slugs" gave an unbelievable non-performance.

⮕◦⬅

Throughout the trial, Tony's mind constantly reverted back to what Uncle Gino had confided in him. Years ago his father had been in the same situation. He had chosen to go to jail, leaving a young wife and child rather than expose the Family. In a sense, Tony had been placed in a similar situation. And he had chosen to honor his own family and protect it. His godfather had not been implicated. Only Bonitto and his henchmen. What Red and Ben didn't know about his Family connections was better left unsaid.

———⇒•○•⇐———

Tony and Ben sat in the assistant DA's office, heads bowed, neither uttering a word. The trial was over, and they had gotten a conviction, but it was obvious neither man was overjoyed.

To Tony, the good news was that he had defied the odds and had not become a statistic. The bad news was so overwhelming it was difficult to rank it on the despair-o-meter. In no special order of seriousness, he had: killed three men in the space of about fifteen minutes (granted it was self-defense and the world would be somewhat better off without them); directly caused the death of a beautiful young woman (this gnawed at him constantly); met the girl of his dreams and lost her before he had had the chance to feel the thrill and passion of courtship; caused his family to be displaced to God knows where; met and lost the first true friend his own age he'd ever known; lost the opportunity of being able to pursue the career he'd prepared for all his life; lost the town he loved so much (not to mention the people who made it so special).

Just when his head and spirits could sink no lower, someone knocked on the office door. A young man came in and handed him a letter.

"Mr. Amico, this was addressed to you and left on the secretary's desk."

"Thanks," said a puzzled Tony, wearily tearing open the end. As he read the short note, a smile appeared for the first time in weeks. He looked up at Ben Griffin and spoke with a voice that was more relaxed than it had been since the whole nightmare began.

"Let's forget about that witness protection program. I don't think I'll be needing it after all."

"Have you lost your mind, Tony? You won't last ten minutes out on the street."

"Let's say I just received my insurance policy." He shook Ben's hand and walked out of the office.

Ben looked down at the note on the table. He picked it up and read.

Anthony, our debt to your father has been paid. Go in peace.
                                                          --A.S

Tony burst outside and looked up at the sky. He took a deep breath as the clear, fresh air flooded his lungs. Stopping abruptly, he saw a black limousine pulling out from the curb. The tinted window slowly lowered, exposing a sight that had haunted his thoughts since that afternoon in Little Italy. The old man's face was expressionless. Only a slight nod and subtle salute to Tony gave any hint of recognition. Before Tony could say anything, the car pulled out into the busy traffic and disappeared.

Epilogue

Tony returned to Chagrin Falls and lost himself in his work at the Stroud-Lawrence Funeral Home. He worked so tirelessly that Don and Judi were able to go on their first extended vacation since they were married. They celebrated by attending the International Morticians Convention in Luxor, Egypt. Don hoped to get some "fresh" ideas but just came back with a lot of stale jokes. Judi returned sporting a Cleopatra coiffeur and a fabulous tan.

Good Shepherd Funeral Home continued to prosper, but the crematorium was demolished. In its place was a beautiful garden where three statues stood among the flowers and foliage. The statues were of the three Scarletto brothers. No one can confirm what is buried under the thick cement foundations. A Japanese conglomerate purchased the business with the understanding that the statues would never be moved.

The Scarlettos now own six Italian bakeries scattered throughout the greater Cleveland area.

Carlo and his boys are still doing hard time and have never uttered a single word since their arrest.

Carley Benton was not at Nighttown when the FBI agent tried to find her. To Tony's chagrin, she was never heard from again. All information obtained from family records confirmed that Terri Benton never had a sister.